William Pri

Sarah J. Waldock

Dedicated to my husband, with whom my first ever conversation was about Hornblower; and to our dear cat Merlin who was always such a help with the keyboard.

Contents

Lieutenant Price of the 'Thrush'

Chapter 1

Lieutenant William Price tried not to tug at the single gold epaulette on his right shoulder where it seemed to sit oddly; it did not in fact sit as unevenly as it felt, but the uniform was so new that it felt strange.

He felt sick; not seasick, but sick with excitement and apprehension in equal measure. It was a feeling he always hoped he would grow out of; but he never had. He had felt the same when he was about to join his first ship; and before his first battle. And the second and third if he was honest with himself. There was no reason for him to be apprehensive – at least, so long as his new captain was not as crazy as Piggot, the captain of the Hermione, who had believed everyone was conspiring against him – but nonetheless his body betrayed him with that queasy feeling and a mouth as dry as if he had been shouting into salt spray. He swallowed hard.

The Thrush's coxwain who was rowing him out to where the 'Thrush' stood out to sea grinned.

"New promotion, Sir?"

"Yes" said William, grinning absurdly. Excitement was winning against apprehension.

"So the Thursday Toast will be your favourite, eh?" said the man slyly.

The Thursday toast – following the loyal toast of course – was for a bloody war or a sickly season; part of the black humour of the Wardroom since either one would ensure rapid promotion. William had never yet been in a wardroom to make the toast but he had been a midshipman long enough to have heard about it.

"Damn your impudence!" he said firmly.

The man grinned unrepentantly.

William was excited and scared both at once because he would have authority now, of which he had had precious little hitherto; and no more must he satisfy the Sailing Master of his mathematical competence or risk a beating over the gun. He was on the path that should lead eventually to his own ship one day – unless he proved incompetent or Boney really WAS defeated as some whispered – and once he could make Post Captain the journey to Admiral depended only on survival.

That of course was a journey with a lot of ifs and buts in it; but for a jubilant young man who had passed his examination in front of the examination board of three captains, who had sworn he was over nineteen – he had written the number on a scrap of paper and placed it in one shoe so he really could truthfully say he was over nineteen – and was found a commission almost straight away by the kind offices of Admiral Crawford such caveats were trivial.

It had made his blood boil that his poor sister Fanny had been duped by Henry Crawford, the Admiral's nephew, into believing that the fellow had any say in making him a lieutenant; why such preferment might occur in the army, but how could Fanny be such a dear little idiot not to realise that the Royal Navy required competence in its officers and no amount of money or preferment would gain real promotion!

The coxswain skilfully manoeuvred the ship's boat up to the ladder from the companion port on the starboard side for William to scramble up with all the skill he could muster – not as easy as had the ship still been in harbour where he had expected to board her – and onto the deck. He came on board with as much grace as he could manage, which was never going to be much coming onto a sloop up a ladder that felt as though it wanted to throw him into the sea.

Doubtless the coxswain, rowing round to the larboard side as a rating must, would manage with more grace. The boat and William's dunnage would be winched on board.

10

He was met by a cheerful looking man some years older than himself also with a single epaulet.

"William Price? I'm Hector Phrayle, first lieutenant" he said.

William saluted.

Phrayle sketched a salute back.

"Let's not stand on too much ceremony" he said "There's only us and the surgeon and the Sailing Master in the wardroom; your first commission?"

"Aye, sir" said William nervously.

"Well I ain't about to make you kiss the gunner's daughter so try not to look like you expect me to" said Phrayle "Come below; your dunnage will soon be with you!"

William followed him down to the wardroom. A couple of sailors were already carrying down his seachest.

"You're on the larboard; direct access to the quarter galley" said Phrayle "Which means if the surgeon drinks and has to void that half the night he'll be tramping through your cabin to use the quarter galley; the gunner shouldn't be a problem and I'm lucky that the Sailing Master, who gets to use the one on my side, is young and hale enough to have a strong bladder. The purser is a sorry specimen but I can live with his furtive trip during the dog watch when I'm below."

"Er, who says the surgeon drinks?" asked William

"Well, it's often known that surgeons drink you know; fail to keep up a practice and so volunteer for the navy, and he's new too. Well, to be honest, I've served with the captain before – Master and Commander properly of course – when we were third and fourth on a frigate. He's a good officer. And the Sailing Master was master's mate of the same ship. Admiral Crawford lets no good deed go unpunished as they say; so for our sins we have our own sweet little bird of a ship and a prayer that Boney gives us some sport for her."

"Amen!" said William happily. "I – er, I owe the commission to Admiral Crawford's kindness. And Mr Campbell the surgeon is known to me as a decent sober man and very pleasant."

"Oh, in that case, my apologies; glad to hear it; we obviously struck lucky! As to the Admiral, he wouldn't have found you a berth if he didn't think you deserved it" said Phrayle "You'd be sweating it out as Passed Midshipman or Master's Mate somewhere if he didn't like the cut of your jib. Now are we going to pull together or are you too ambitious to be the third of three officers and are looking to cause me grief?"

"Oh NO sir!" said William "I might have passed my exams but there's an awful lot to learn still!"

Phrayle grinned.

"You'll do laddie" he said "And the name's Hector off duty. The officer of the watch right now is a beardless snotty named Thomas Jenkinson who is actually as serious as he looks; I always distrust a sober-minded appearing midshipmen until proven innocent. The other two brats are technically captain's servants; Prescott is twelve, Lord, who's just come aboard, is eleven. Prescott is a small demon and Lord looks like he still wets his hammock and is like to cry at anything."

"I have a brother about his age" said William, thinking of Sam.

"What, volunteering to be the snotties' nursemaid? Good man…. Brigham's a good fellow – that's the sailing master – he's stern with the young gentlemen but he won't bully them unnecessarily. Everett – bosun – is a sour creature but fair. If he starts any man, you can be sure that man deserves it. And Porkins the gunner has a bark worse than his bite with the boys"

"Thanks" said William. Getting an insight into the senior ratings was an added bonus that not all first lieutenants would have volunteered. "And – and I don't mind hearing some of the lessons of the young gentlemen; though I have not the most extensive of educations myself."

"Ah, excellent; anything to keep them out of mischief – and keep an eye on their wellbeing" said Phrayle. "It means a bit of extra pay for you too, which I'm guessing you won't pass up! We should have a happy enough ship then – once we've licked the crew into order. It's why we moved rather than waiting on your arrival; Captain Mornington was concerned we might find some swimming ashore to run. We've the usual bunch of gaolbirds of course; a few pressed; and half a dozen picked men, including the cox'n. Cheeky blighter, ain't he?"

"He, er, did seem a little free in his manner" said William.

"Well whatever he says in private as it were, he's loyal enough" said Phrayle. "So, I'll leave you to settle into your new home; Cap'n told me to get the ship under way as soon as you were aboard."

"Where are we bound?" asked William.

"South" said Phrayle "Other than that? Sealed orders; none of my business."

He left William in the tiny cabin – even so, almost eight foot by eight foot all to himself was a kingly amount of space compared to his midshipman's berth – to sort out his sea chest. The officer's cot hung from the deck beams above; and he had a tiny bit of the sternlight for light as well as the door to the quarter gallery where he might relieve himself at will. The cannon took up a significant part of his cabin it was true; and when they were at quarters the screen that made up the wall of his cabin would come down to allow the men to get to it to fire it. But it was a cabin of his own!

And as he felt the lurch of the sails being released and taking wind in them and heard the wind thrumming in the rigging and the creak of the planking he thrilled with the thought that he was soon to be at sea – as a lieutenant!

Chapter 2

William knocked at the door of the captain's cabin and heard a slightly strangled command to enter. When he went in, his hat under his arm, and saluted, the captain was busy tying his stock in the rather inadequate mirror. He was a man in his late twenties with a rugged, weatherbeaten face and twinkling blue eyes below prematurely thinning hair of a nondescript colour.

"Ah, Lieutenant Price" said Captain Edgar Mornington "You will excuse me not being fully dressed; I felt the ship go under way and got up. Lt Phrayle and I have been standing watch and watch for the last few days; we have a few mutinous dogs on board."

William went scarlet.

"I – I'm sorry sir! If I'd known I'd have cut short my leave.....I wanted to see my family...."

The captain cut short his stammering apology with a wave of the hand.

"My dear fellow of course you did; nothing to worry about. And now you're here it will be a great relief. At sea, nothing wrong with the Sailing Master standing a watch too, but I didn't want that level of responsibility on the poor fellow in port when they were more likely to try something. We have the leavings of the gaols. Bit of a baptism of fire for you my dear boy; but I'm sure you'll be equal to it. So off you hop and relieve Phrayle and tell him to take a watch below. I've had a couple of hours sleep so I'm fresh enough; I'll be catching up on my paperwork so if you're concerned call down through the skylight and I'll come up" he smiled "I doubt you'll need me but I recall feeling that it was nice to know that there was a senior officer on call just in case."

"Th-thank you sir!" said William who did appreciate it; and appreciated more that the captain made it clear that it was not fear of his incompetence but to give him confidence that he had said it.

A couple of hours sleep and feeling fresh! The captain was a superman; a hero!

William Price gave his loyalty to Edgar Mornington in that short conversation.

He went on deck where he was finally able to start to get some idea about his new home, after passing to Lt Phrayle the captain's compliments and the order to take a watch below.

Phrayle had grinned and said he would not object!

The Thrush was a well found looking little ship, trim in her lines – as he had seen on approaching her – with her masts looking well balanced to her length. Of course a sloop of war was a tiny vessel even compared to a frigate, and never mind even comparing her to the big first and second raters, next to which she was a washing tub. From the quarterdeck a hail even without a megaphone would readily reach the bows no matter how much other activity was going on, the slapping sound of running bare feet as the sailors went to their tasks not drowning out the sound on so small a vessel.

The sails flogged rather; William frowned. The topmen were slow getting them reefed up properly; but then much of the ship's company were green so it would not do to expect miracles. Nor would it do to let the men get in the habit of sloppy seamanship.

"Aloft! Get those sails properly trimmed!" he called.

Topmen swarmed out along the yards high above him to obey his orders; slower than a well regulated company, though some looked to know what they were doing.

He turned to the jovial looking man by the wheel. He was perhaps the shady side of forty; it was hard to tell. His moon-shaped face was unlined but his eyes held experience.

"Sailing Master?" he asked.

"Aye, sir; John Brigham's my name. If I might say, you were perfectly correct to hurry them to that. We'll be coming round a point in half an hour too so you'll have the opportunity of watching the useless lot in action. Captain's planning exercises while we sail south; to bring 'em up to speed and to keep 'em too tired to try any monkey-tricks."

"Sounds good," said William, "William Price; not long promoted. I, er, I hope you'll give me any hints I need," he added.

Brigham gave a broad grin.

"That I will sir; and not where any sailor can hear them either, or at least not so's he'd know I was hinting. Watch out for that sly looking fellow down there; Scully his name is, and it's a cully he is. Sea Lawyer IF you like; one of our gaolbirds and if you ask me probably one as cooked the books and wouldn't think twice about slitting the weasand of anyone who found him out at it. He's articulate he is; full of fine speeches. Born to be hanged."

"I fancy if he tries to organise a mutiny, he will be," said William, "if he doesn't slit our weasands first. He does look a real villain. Or rather he looks like he'd like to see us all supping with Neptune."

"Cox'n has his eye on him" said Brigham. "If they try anything my money's on it being once the landlubbers have got over their seasickness and are finding their way about without aching in places they didn't know they had places; so about a week."

"I am sure you are right" said William. "I hope that the Captain's plan of keeping them busy works."

Brigham grinned.

"Well if nothing else it should teach the lubbers how to do their jobs. He'll be running competitions, Port and Larboard watches against each other. The old hands – and we have yet to find out who of them are reliable as well as handy – are split, and it'll be up to them to show the new hands what to do, if only because they want their prizes. The captain guessed how it was going to be and he has small prizes, baccy and tea and coffee for the watches that do well. Better a carrot for an ass than a stick."

"Yes, I can see that" said William "If we have gaolbirds though, we'll have to watch out for thievery."

Brigham spat over the side.

"Most men despise those who steal from their own" he said "There'll either be some unofficial poundings of the offenders or they'll give 'em up quick enough for flogging by reporting the theft and making sure the officers can figure out who done it."

William nodded.

"I see" he said. "I have a lot to learn."

Brigham chuckled, not unkindly.

"Big step from being a snotty with relatively little in the way of responsibility – because any captain sending a snotty off on a prize makes sure he has steady men – and having to deal with real problems" he said "If you'll pardon me saying so, sir, an officer who recognises that he needs to learn more has a better chance of living to do so."

"Thank you" said William "I don't take that amiss at all; in fact I shall greatly value your advice."

"Watch the Captain" said Brigham "That's the best advice you could have; this is his first official command but he's been prize captain many times, and never got command before because he's unconventional and hadn't got the patronage until Admiral Crawford took an interest in him. And the captain picked Mr Phrayle and me and Yarde the cox'n and Porkins the gunner. And the Admiral gave us some choice able seamen and the surgeon so with luck...... anyhow, the captain is as good a man to copy as any. And on seamen and seamanship, well, you just ask and I'll give you what I know, son – er, sir."

William nodded.

"Very good" he said. Asking advice was one thing but he had to keep a distance even so between his commission and the warranted men, even the Sailing Master.

And Brigham agreed for he nodded approval at the use of official words.

"Is it your wish sir that we come up a point now?" asked the sailing master.

He was glancing at the sea and at the sails, beginning to flog as they cleared the lee of the land.

"Indeed it is" said William. "LAY ALOFT THERE AND STAND BY TO COME UP A POINT!" he bellowed.

The sailors swarmed up the ratlines and out onto the yards in preparation as William delivered the series of orders that soon had the sails trimmed as the ship wore round to a subtly new heading.

It was slow and clumsy. Evolutions at sea were definitely called for.

When William came off watch he called the midshipmen to him.

"Very well, you scrubs, I've volunteered as schoolmaster to you; but I think a bit of seamanship is going to be more important to start off with than Latin and any more mathematics than the sailing master give you" he said, absently grabbing small dark haired Lord and swinging him out of the way of an encroaching but concealed point "I saw that, Mr Prescott, and if you think it's funny to wound a comrade with your dirk – which you shouldn't even have yet as you're not warranted until you're thirteen – then you've a very odd sense of humour"

The boy with reddish hair and large ears flushed.

"I was only going to prick him sir to wake him up."

"And that's not a wound? What if the ship rolls – like that" as the sea heaved its seventh wave – "And makes a bigger cut? What if it goes septic as wounds at sea often do? What if he has to have the leg amputated for that? What if he dies having it amputated? You aspire to be an officer and a gentleman; if you must play tricks on a boy very much younger and smaller than yourself because you're too cowardly to pick on anyone else, try at least for some semblance of thought to make them safe tricks. Now let us repair to the cannon and consider some of its attributes and actions" said William, satisfied that worse consequences had never presented themselves to Colin Prescott whose red face spoke of having been sufficiently disciplined in being made to consider them. William wanted the boys near to the man Scully; a discontented looking man with intelligent eyes that burned with resentment. He wanted to see if a clever man would eavesdrop.

"We've drawn the gun sir, and learned which ones fire what weight of ball" piped Lord.

"A start" said William. "You are the youngest; you will learn most by listening to me questioning the knowledge of your more experienced fellows. Mr Jenkins!" he addressed the oldest boy, also dark of hair and serious of manner. "What is the first thing you do when the cannon has been fired?"

"Reload it sir" said Jenkins promptly.

"Are you certain?" asked William.

Jenkins looked puzzled; then nodded his tousled head emphatically.

"Aye sir" he said.

"I fear, Mr Jenkins, if that is your level of gunnery skill, you cannot know your tampion from a Norfolk pompion" William said. "Don't you think you ought to do something else first?"

Mr Lord was jumping up and down.

"You wash it out!" he squeaked.

"You have to bring it inboard first" said Prescott.

"The recoil will bring it inboard, though quite right to consider that," said William, "and it will stop against the breaching – the rope that passes through the ring here on the casca bell at the breech. And then as Mr Lord says you swab out. WHY do you swab out?"

"OH!" said Jenkins as it dawned on him "In case any incompletely burned powder from the charge is still inside smouldering because when you put in the next charge it could explode."

"Exactly" said William "And as officers your job is to learn how to best *preserve* the lives of your men, not put them at risk. This is why we shall be practising until everyone aboard is fit to drop, not just at gunnery but at sail handling; because if we run into a storm at sea, or have to flee from a bigger ship it's a bit late then to start learning how to handle the sails efficiently, isn't it?"

"Aye sir" said Jenkins.

William could see Scully out of the corner of his eye, listening.

"Some of our newer hands will find it hard to understand and accept that" said William "They didn't ask to be here! But I think when they are skilled it has to be a better life than many."

"I didn't ask to be here either, sir!" said Prescott "My pa said that as I was a second son I should be for the sea and as I let my pet rat bite the housekeeper I should go young!"

"Well I can't say as I think much of that as a punishment" said William "I came to sea at thirteen which is quite young enough in my opinion. You should in that case think how much worse is the lot of the powder monkeys indentured out of foundling hospitals and hardly any chance at prize money rather than taking out your anger on your father by playing silly tricks as I suspect you do. You are nominally an officer and a gentleman; do please try to live up to it."

"Please sir, may I be excused then? I – I am ashamed of having… well it was a trick I played on the ship's boys."

"Then you may be excused to undo it; you show manliness in owning to it and seeing the error of your ways" said William, surprised and pleased that his homily had made Prescott think!

The boy would doubtless be a small imp of mischief but if he could at least refrain from playing tricks on those who could not retaliate it would stop some misery from unintentional bullying. Discipline in the dangerous environment of a fighting ship had to be taut, and an officer, even a nominal one like a snotty, had to be backed up and had to be obeyed by the hands, and was immune from their retaliation. It could lead to some quite dreadful abuses, and William had once fought another midshipman called Arbuckle for issuing unreasonable orders that meant that the other boy could order punishment for failure to perform his orders. They had both been beaten for fighting of course; but the other boy had stopped his blatant bullying for fear of William who had managed to use the dirty fighting he had learned growing up in a rough neighbourhood to hurt Arbuckle quite a lot.

He questioned the other two about loading and firing the cannons, and put similar questions to Prescott when the boy returned, and finally dismissed them to write for him a brief report on the same. They pulled faces; but William said,

"You will one day thank me; when you have to report to the admiralty what actions you took, the clarity of how you write might one day be the difference between being gazetted or being court martialled."

They went off with long faces; but William knew they would do it.

And Scully was still listening.

Chapter 3

The evolutions were not popular; but William was relieved that there was less muttering than there might have been. Captain Mornington announced that there would be no racing until the new hands had been given a fair chance to literally know the ropes; and that gunnery drill would be done slowly and by the numbers until every man knew his task and that the old hands must bear with the new ones to avoid undue accident.

William saw Scully nod to himself when the captain said that and gave a brief prayer of thanks that the captain was of a like mind to himself in that.

He hesitated; and asked the captain if he might have a word; and explained what he had done.

"He seems intelligent sir; if he has some reasons for what we do given to him, I thought it might be easier than having to break him as a mutineer."

In truth, William had seen in Scully's eyes something that reminded him of one of the seamen punished by the boy Arbuckle and pushed to the limit of endurance. The man had deserted and had been caught and hanged, the final straw which had pushed William into fighting. He always reproached himself that he had not acted sooner, whereby the man might not have felt that he had no choice but to run. He had now the opportunity to act sooner where Scully was concerned.

Edgar Mornington clapped William on the shoulder.

"My dear boy! You never did a better piece of work! I know Brigham is ready to believe him capable of murdering us in our beds – and maybe if he were picked on all the time and desperate that would be true – but if you can win his confidence then we might have ourselves a potential asset. Frankly if he pulls his weight and learns the trade I'd look to giving any intelligent man a letter of recommendation for a warrant."

"Thank you sir; you do not then mind if I make him something of a – a project?"

"Laddie, if you can stop the cleverest gaolbird aboard from turning mutineer and make him instead an asset to the fleet – even if it's only as a purser – you go ahead with my blessing so long as it doesn't interfere with your other duties. You can send for him to wait on the young gentlemen doing lessons below if you think that his eavesdropping is doing him and therefore the ship any good."

"Thank you sir" said William, much relieved. "I know it was an unwarrantable cheek to interfere; I just saw an opportunity."

Mornington laughed.

"Yes, that's why it's taken me so long to get my command" he said "Unwarrantable cheek and taking opportunities; some of which came off, some of which did not, and one which embarrassed a senior captain who had declared a task impossible. He had influence; I did not. Never stop taking opportunities my boy; unless you decided to ride out your career in safety."

William grinned.

"Somehow I don't think that's very likely sir" he said.

"Well, hop off to your classes; and if you think Scully wants to talk ask him to give you a hand brushing up your dress uniform. I'm inviting the officers, surgeon and sailing master to dinner tonight."

Scully stood by the table in the Midshipman's berth with a flagon of wine and heaved a sigh as little Lord made a mess of the basic Latin that William felt he ought to be helping the boys to acquire.

"Scully, do you read Latin?" William asked.

"Yes – I mean, aye sir" said Scully.

"Then put that damn flagon down in the middle of the table and give Mr Lord a hand; he's in need of a lot of catching up" said William.

"Aye sir. Beg pardon, why do the young gentlemen need Latin?" asked Scully. William read a genuine puzzlement and a desire to know.

"Because they are supposed to get an education commensurate with that of any young gentleman which means too that they should have a passing knowledge of how to unravel legal documents" said William "And no, it's not as important as seamanship but as they have started to learn at school it seems a shame to let it go rusty; and it's a basis for both French and Spanish as well as Italian."

"I know French sir if you were wishful to have it taught" Scully blurted out.

"That's an excellent idea" said William "And I should like to learn more myself for I only know a little; and if the captain cannot find a way the young gentlemen and I will chip in to pay for your services in that. I don't believe for one moment that we have all but seen the back of Boney. You will have permission to issue reprimand for inattention so long as you append 'sir' to every vituperation."

Scully actually grinned; it made his narrow weasel like face almost attractive.

That was going well.

After the Latin lesson – and Lord seemed to be picking it up well with extra help from a man, William thought, with more knowledge of the language than himself – Scully effaced himself in the corner again whilst William lectured on the sails and how they worked.

"Because the Sloop is small we have only two masts; we have a mainmast and a mizzen or rear mast; and the mizzen is fore-and-aft rigged. This makes us quite manoeuvrable; I personally consider it a more manoeuvrable configuration than having a mainmast fitted with the fore-and-aft sail instead of a course, rigged as our mizzen is, and regular sails on a foremast. I always think the ships rigged thus look a little sluggish by the bow and are harder to trim. 'Thrush' used to be 'La Merle' a French sloop and one can see it in her cleaner lines that a British ship."

"Sir, isn't that unpatriotic?" asked Jenkins.

"No, Mr Jenkins: it's a matter of fact," said William, "and the American ships are even better in their design; if you ever read the 'Naval Chronicle' you will see that plaint has been made of this to the admiralty when the sloop 'Avon' was taken by the American brig-sloop 'Wasp'. The Jonathons know how to build ships; and their sloops outgun ours. We have thirteen guns and a complement of almost fifty men; most of their sloops have eighteen guns and over an hundred men. If an American vessel came upon us today – not impossible since they have been so bold as to attack our shipping in the Irish sea, with most of our fleet involved blockading Brest, we would not stand a chance though of course we would fight. American privateers would show no mercy for our hands being green."

"Do they slaughter prisoners sir?" asked Lord, nervously.

"No lad; at least, I should say *most* do not; there are after all those privateers little better than pirates. But I suspect that a bloody engagement to reduce the numbers of prisoners they have to take would be a course to be taken" said William. "However, let us get back to the business of the sails; so that if we are approached by an American vessel we might know enough about our sails to outrun her; no shame in living to fight another day when hopelessly outgunned."

"Couldn't we use a – a ruse de guerre and pretend to be French to get away as it's a French ship?" asked Prescott.

"A good point, Mr Prescott; and the sort of thought that sorts out the officers who survive and go on to become Post Captains so long as they mind their lessons in the meantime" said William who had decided that Prescott needed any praise tempered with firm squashing!

Having little brothers certainly made dealing with lively midshipmen easier; though William considered that his whole family were done no favours by their mother's weak discipline. He had been shocked at how the younger boys ran riot and how spoiled Betsey was! Tom and Charles would find it particularly hard to adapt to discipline afloat if they joined the Navy.

The lesson proceeded smoothly as he explained how the fore-and-aft rig worked, and the need for the vang, the heavy cable running from the fore-and-aft sail to the ring on the quarterdeck to prevent the boom from rising up under the pressure of the wind. He also explained that many sailors pronounced it 'wang' so that they should not be confused hearing it so called.

"Why sir?" predictably Prescott wanted to know.

"I'm not sure," said William, honestly, "but I suspect it's something to do with the rig having come first from Flanders and the Dutch way of pronouncing things that got 'corrected' by English sailors or some such. It isn't because of the way we pronounce 'v' in Latin" he added. That raised a laugh from the boys!

"Might I ask some things sir?" asked Scully, lingering as the boys scattered in relief to put away their books.

"Certainly, Scully; but come to my cabin to ask; I have to prepare my dress uniform to dine with the captain" said William. "Perhaps you will give me a hand."

"Aye sir" said Scully. He followed William and as soon as they were in the after cabin he burst out,

"It's this way sir; I'm a man of letters not a man accustomed to labour. And it doesn't seem fair that I've fetched up the lowest of the low here."

"Actually de facto on ship the younger Gentlemen are the lowest of the low, they just have to be called sir if a seaman curses them" said William. "No I doubt it does seem fair. I understand you're from the gaol?"

Scully flushed.

"Yes sir; one slip! One temptation!"

"Would you like to tell me about it?" asked William "Oh I am so glad not to be on Jamaica station; the *mould*!" as he shook out his uniform. He turned to look at Scully so the man knew he had his attention. Scully swallowed, then spoke in a low, intense voice.

"My mother was ill. I forged a small legacy onto the bottom of a will, a gratuity to the clerks of the solicitor handling it" he said. "It would have meant nothing to the man's estate; and would have paid for a good doctor for my mother. But one of the other clerks saw me doing something clandestine and he spoke to the senior clerk."

"I see," said William, "technically theft but I don't say that if it were my mother, or one of my siblings I might not have done the same. Your mother?"

"She died sir," said Scully, "with me in gaol and nobody to care for her."

"That's harsh," said William, "I am sorry."

"You know sir," Scully sounded awed, "I believe you really are!"

"I am" said William. "I am fortunate in having a large family and knowing there would be someone to care for *my* mother. What was it that you hoped I might do?"

Scully twisted long fingers together.

"Well, it's this road sir; I'd like to do something that uses my skills."

William nodded.

"I see" he said. "I can see two paths for you in the Navy, Scully, in which you use their skills; one uses them right away but has little opportunity to rise; the other is the harder path but has more potential."

"What are they, sir?"

"Well the first is to be assigned Purser's mate; and with certificates of competency from him be warranted as a purser.   The captain is ready to give letters of recommendation to any man intelligent enough to deserve a warrant.   The second path is to study seamanship and apply when you have been rated able seaman and then bosun as Master's Mate; whereat you might aspire to be Sailing Master, which has the chance of a small command of your own: or to take the even harder step – since it would bring misunderstanding because of your age – of applying to be a midshipman and serve three years to become a lieutenant. The rules for a lieutenant are that the man must be over nineteen; and have served at sea at least six years three of which are to have been as midshipman. I went to sea as a snotty at thirteen. I've done my six years; you look at me and feel it unfair that a man some, what, four, five years your junior should be so much above you; but I've worked for it."

"I see sir" said Scully, abashed "It's good of you to be so frank with me."

"Scully, if you were the ordinary cut of seaman and gaolbird I shouldn't be" said William "I'm relying on your intelligence and sense of fairness to recognise that I'm unbending because you're *not* in the common mould – and because one day we might serve together as fellow officers if you have the bottom to go for it."

Scully nodded.

"I'll go for it" he said.

"In which case you may borrow my copy of the Manual of Seamanship that I studied from" said William. "I have permission for you to wait on the young gentlemen and learn by listening; but I am going to lay on you the order that you do not disturb discipline by asking questions at the time but note them down – I will see that you have paper and a pen – to ask me later."

"Sir, you've put yourself out for me; and I confess I was ready to rouse up the others in mutiny because I know I could" said Scully.

"Yes; I was fairly sure you could," said William calmly, "and it seemed a shame and a waste that a clever man should end up getting himself hanged when a little bit of trouble could show you a way to reconcile yourself with this apparent setback."

"Thank you sir!" said Scully clutching the book that William handed him and thrusting out a hand.

William put forward his own automatically and Scully shook it firmly.

"It's bad discipline as it stands" said William gently "But I understand."

Scully had no other way to express his gratitude; William knew that.

The man nodded firmly; and darted away to his own hammock. This was a way out of the trap he found himself in; to use the intellect he had to move on, and make the best of it. Scully was under no illusions that mutiny would end in being hanged sooner or later; and that the bitterness that almost did not care so long as he struck out at symbols of the authority that were part of life's inequalities was a foolishness when another way was offered to him. For the first time in he could not recall how long, Scully felt that the trap was maybe opening a little to give him a glimpse of working towards freeing himself.

Chapter 4

"The King!"

The captain's guests drank the loyal toast after having dined on a well cooked haricot of mutton served with a dish of carling peas well peppered and roast onions and roast carrots cooked in a Dutch Oven besides. It would never have been considered more than a mean meal to any society host, but was certainly an improvement on the usual salt pork or salt beef with the peas boiled as a pottage and eked out with oatmeal, and any other vegetables that might be available all boiled in together too. William knew that Captain Mornington had paid out of his own pocket for barrels of sauerkraut, unpopular with the men but a means of combating the ever-present risk of scurvy.

"And now, gentlemen, the orders under which we sail" said Captain Mornington. "And tough ones too. You have all read in the 'Naval Chronicle' about the taking of the 'Avon'. The Jonathons are a wasteful lot; I know that their ships are superior to ours but their habit of scuttling every ship they take is a crying shame."

"Perhaps sir, it's an act of calculated contempt" said Phrayle.

"I wouldn't say you're wrong, Hector" said the captain. "The Americans seem to take delight in pulling our noses; like their raids into the Irish sea. And it is said that one of their privateers has made half a dozen forays and has already taken goods to the value of a million of their dollars."

Campbell whistled.

"A dollar is worth about five shillings..... that's a quarter of a million pounds! That's incredible!"

"Quite" said Mornington. "Which being so, the Admiralty wants to play the game of beans for peas; our orders are to take by any means we may an American privateer to return to Britain – and NOT burn it so that their nose may be rubbed into it wearing the Union Flag."

"If it were anyone but you, sir, I should say out of hand that it was impossible" said Phrayle.

"*Ruse de guerre!*" said William excited.

"Mr Price? Expand on that?" said the captain.

"Sir, I was discussing the Americans, and in fact the 'Avon', earlier with the boys," said William, "and saying that there was no shame in running to fight another day from a greater force. And young Prescott suggested wearing French colours as it's a French built ship to be ignored by the Jonathons. I just thought; could we take that a step further and sail into an American port to cut out a brig-sloop that has half its men ashore on liberty?"

There was a long silence.

"I *like* the way you think young William" said Mornington.

"It was Prescott's idea" said William.

"No; the initial thought of disguise was Prescott's. The idea of using it offensively was yours. The thing is we need French speakers. D'ye speak French, William?"

"A little" said William "I planned to engage Scully to teach me more – and the boys too."

"*SCULLY?*" Brigham was horrified into raising his voice.

"He's resentful" said William "And clever. If he's using his brains he resents less. I'm prepared to pay for my own lessons if he can't be logged and rated for it."

"If he'll teach French I guarantee we're likely to use it" said Mornington. "I've no objection so long as he takes orders from any of his pupils out of class. Is he fluent?"

"I had not ascertained sir" said William "However he is a better man at Latin than I am; and as he offered French without hesitation I think one may assume he is fluent enough to feel confident at imparting his knowledge. I noticed that he was impatient that Mr Lord was stumbling and asked him to help the lad; Mr Lord was doing very well under individual tutelage. I know it is irregular; and I beg your pardon Mr Brigham, but I think he will do well for being given some trust."

"From what I have seen of him since Mr Price has used cunning to let Scully overhear some truths Scully is a fast learner and willing to accept and return trust" said Mornington.

"He has been less truculent" said Phrayle "When he came on watch he saluted me willingly and listened most carefully to the instructions I offered. But rather than single him out I think perhaps we should ask for French speaking volunteers to be those men who are visible – if I take the idea correctly?"

"You do, Hector" said Mornington "The advantage of having worked together. Mr Brigham, can you find an objection?"

"Well the fellow has been more willing" said Brigham slowly. "But calling for volunteers ain't such a bad idea. I don't know no French sir, I'm afraid."

"Fortunately I do" said Mornington "Hector you have some?"

"Only enough to ask for the price of a jug of wine, bread and cheese and a night with a whore" said Phrayle. "Never envisioning ever needing any more."

Campbell chuckled.

"You only need two words for that – *de combien*, how much, and a finger to point with."

"Good grief man, don't give away *all* my secrets!" laughed Phrayle who had taken to Campbell once he started to get to know him.

Campbell grinned.

"I have some French, sir" he told the captain "I learned some from school and the rest from trying to make up to my sister's French Canadian governess."

"I can just see the face of the Captain of the American vessel" murmured Mornington "When you go up to him and say 'Ah, my little cabbage, you fill me with delight, I should like to kiss your hands, your neck your face, my heart which is larger than the pen of my uncle yet smaller than the garden of my aunt, overflows.'"

There was much hilarity, Campbell being the first to start laughing.

"It would be quite a moment" agreed Campbell. "Somehow the words *'je t'adore'* were NOT ones I had planned on using!"

"Really," said Mornington, "all we need is for there to be some French conversation going on that sounds authentic and which, should the Jonathons have a French speaker, is not out of place. A couple of seamen or seeming seamen discussing the potential merits of all those things seamen everywhere discuss – the booze and the women. Orders given in the French tongue. Which orders will have to be learned by rote by the seamen handling sails" he pulled a face.

"Beg pardon sir, but as they must learn sail handling from scratch anyway, many of them, why not attach numbers to the orders – and then teach French numbers?" said William "Easier to learn than a string of French orders and after all, who knows what the French might do – they already changed the calendar to make it more supposedly efficient."

"Phrayle, check the boy's brains aren't about to catch fire," said Mornington, "he's full of ideas today! I like that, William; and I have a few ideas of my own. In fact, you can teach Brigham here the numbers and he can include them in French as well as English right from the word go."

Brigham groaned but nodded.

"I think," said William, "I had better teach you how to say them without showing you the words written down. Some of them are pronounced very strangely."

"Comes of being French" growled Brigham. "What d'ye expect, sir, of people who eat garlic, frogs and snails not to mention horse!"

The ship was travelling at night under furled sails like a merchantman; not, as the captain said, in anywise seamanlike but with more than half their complement of men still rated 'landsman' and it being all too true, not having passed any of the tests towards being rated 'ordinary seaman' then it increased the risk to them and to the ship to have them lay out on the yards at night to deal with a sudden change of wind. Any accident would only increase the resentment levels of the tired, aching, hand-sore landsmen and would mean they were less likely to do their best; and Mornington was a man who preferred to draw his men out than drive them on with fear. With so small a complement as the crew of a sloop it also made no sense to spend lives by driving them on and making falls more likely.

They went to quarters at dawn as was standard; and if the response was slow, there was at least a bit more of an air of the men knowing what they were about.

There were still some grumblers however, and the boson's rattan cane swished down on a couple of shoulders.

And better that, thought William, than that there should have to be official notice taken and a flogging take place. His hero was Lord Cochrane, now with the fleet off the shores of America, who declared that flogging spoiled a good man and made a bad one worse. Even so for some offences – stealing from fellows for example, or risking the lives of all by hoarding the tot and being drunk on watch – it was unavoidable; and that the seamen accepted as fair.

The courses had to be set then of course; and William stood beside Brigham, shouting out the numbers of the orders in French as Brigham gave the order in English.

Scully was on this watch at the moment and gave William a sharp look.

It was not long before William heard one of the seamen telling the other that they were being trained to steal half the fleet at Brest.

When the watch ended – and incidentally William became officially officer of the next watch – he saw Scully collect up a group of the landsmen and start laboriously working through knots with them.

He nodded to himself. With the aid of the book, Scully was not only going to teach himself but also automatically pick up the role of a warrant officer in teaching others.

It might help to make teaching their landsmen how to sail a bit easier.

There was another landsman, a big ox of a fellow with more low cunning, William thought, than intelligence who seemed intent on disrupting this, demanding to know what they were doing and why.

Scully answered him quietly enough that learning more would make duties less difficult and painful; he and his group were given a short burst of language so foul William did not even know the meaning of half the words.

"Bunch o' officers' mollys you" growled the big man – William thought his name was Wick, having heard it on the bosun's lips shouting at him – "You caved in quick enow!"

"Well leaving aside you foul imputations, maybe I felt that it was better to learn to make the best of it than be hanged as a mutineer" said Scully.

"Well I say you is wrong," said Wick, "and him as stays learnin' from you is a molly and not a man. You and your flash lingo!"

"Don't take any notice of the big lug" said Scully to his group.

Several of them got up and moved away from him however; and Everett the bosun moved forward, cane twitching.

"What's going on?" he asked.

"Some of us are practising knots, Mr Everett" said Scully "Perhaps you'd tell us if we are doing it correctly."

Everett regarded him with suspicion.

"I ain't never come across landsmen gaolbirds wot was keen before" he said suspiciously.

"We're keen on not gettin' yore cane more'n we 'as ter" said one of Scully's followers "Can't see as there's anyfink odd in that!"

Everett considered; and nodded.

"Well I can accept that" he said. "Awright, I'll check yer work. Wick, are yer tyin' knots or jus' getting in the light?"

Wick drifted away; but the look he gave Scully made William hope that Scully's disciples would stand by him.

It was the next day that Scully and Wick were brought before the Captain for fighting, Scully pulling away from the bosun's mate to speak to William who signed to the bosun's mate to permit it.

"Mr Price, your book got torn! I'm so sorry, I don't know if it'll mend, we were taken up by the bosun before I could check!"

William nodded.

"Thank you for telling me" he said "I don't blame you Scully; I can guess what happened. Mr Lord! Down below decks if you please, and take to my cabin the torn book – it's the Manual of Seamanship, you'll recognise it – and I'll see what I can do."

"Thank you sir; I can bear a flogging if I know you don't blame me" said Scully as little Lord scuttled off on his errand.

The captain heard both sides – Scully refused to speak and Wick blamed Scully and declared him to be a molly to the officers and was busy declaring his disgust for such practises with a vigour that had Mornington wonder if Wick had ever indeed ever considered the forbidden practice himself that he should protest so much.

Hands were mustered aft to witness punishment.

There was much surprise amongst the old hands; normally if a flogging was to be awarded the culprits would lay up in the brig overnight while the bosun made up a fresh 'cat' for each flogging, splicing the nine tails and covering the handle with red baize and making the baize bag to keep it in. This information spread amongst the new hands too and they waited to see what was to be happening.

"These two men have been fighting" said Mornington "Which is against the King's Regulations. Article twenty two covers it: 'If any person in the fleet shall quarrel or fight with any other person in the fleet, or use reproachful or provoking speeches or gestures, tending to make any quarrel or disturbance, he shall, upon being convicted thereof, suffer such punishment as the offence shall deserve, and a court martial shall impose'. It is hard to get to the bottom of this as only they, and those around them, really know exactly what happened. An officer's property appears to have been damaged at the same time; a book loaned by Lieutenant Price to a literate man who was to help those of his fellows as wished to learn a little more seamanship as so many of you are lubbers. Under the circumstances the prisoners, John Scully and William Wicks are to run the gauntlet of their messmates who are to be issued with knittles of rope ends; since their messmates will known best who is the most to blame or if either are equally to blame. Strike as hard as you feel necessary lads; the gauntlet will be run three times each."

Chapter 5

The gauntlet involved the two messes – fourteen men in total as two of their number were being punished – lining up in two rows, each with a knittle or rope yarn plaited with a half-hitch tied in one end. The captain had ordered the bosun to prepare a number of these as he preferred gauntleting to flogging where possible. The master at arms proceeded the man to be punished, walking backwards with his cutlass at the man's chest, the corporal following with his cutlass while the man sentenced to the gauntlet walked down the lines as his shipmates laid into him with their knittles. Wicks and Scully were ordered to remove their shirts; and Scully was sent to walk up and down the required three times first. William thought it merciful of the captain to let the more imaginative man get it over with.

Though some of Wicks' mess struck hard it was apparent that Scully received relatively little in the way of hard blows in his walk; even some of Wicks' mess being at most half hearted. The men knew where the blame lay.

Wicks on the other hand received the full attention of the seamen who knew full well who had torn the lieutenant's book and started the quarrel.

He was a tough man; and took his beating with little more than the odd grunt; he was plainly furious.

Captain Mornington summoned both men before him.

"I don't want either of you fighting again" he said "If you do I'll consider transferring both of you to separate ships next time we make harbour. There are other ways to avoid conflict" here he looked at Scully who nodded. The captain went on, "And I would also remind anyone who cannot settle of article 19: 'If any person in the fleet shall conceal any traitorous or mutinous practice or design, being convicted thereof by the sentence of a court martial, he shall suffer death, or any other punishment as a court martial shall think fit; and if any person, in or belonging to the fleet, shall conceal any traitorous or mutinous words spoken by any, to the prejudice of His Majesty or government, or any words, practice, or design, tending to the hindrance of the service, and shall not forthwith reveal the same to the commanding officer, or being present at any mutiny or sedition, shall not use his utmost endeavours to suppress the same, he shall be punished as a court martial shall think he deserves.' That means any rising against the lawful officers of this ship; Wick, do I make myself clear?"

Wick scowled.

"Yes sir" he muttered.

"Very good. Try to recall it should be 'aye sir' at sea" said Mornington.

"Please sir, why sir?" asked Scully.

"Because 'aye' can be heard better in a high wind; a sibilant 'yes' can be lost" said Mornington, correctly interpreting the question as a genuine desire to know.

"Thank you sir" said Scully.

Wick muttered something about sucking up.

"Wick" said Mornington "I know who caused the fight. Your fellows confirmed my belief. Stir up any more trouble and I will have you scrubbing the heads from now until doomsday. You are a lucky man because I prefer to avoid flogging. Try to appreciate your good fortune and stay out of trouble – I may be talking to myself but perhaps your fellows will dissuade you from causing too much trouble."

Wick spat on the deck.

The bosun kicked his feet out from under him.

"Clean that up!" he said.

"Thank you Mr Everett" said Mornington. "Scully, dismissed; Mr Everett, carry on."

"Aye aye sir" Everett saluted and Mornington strolled aft listening to Everett's coarse assessment of Wick's character, antecedents, morals and cleanliness alongside a lecture on how lucky he was to have a captain that hadn't ordered three dozen for that offence of impudence and that Wick could find life made very unpleasant if he didn't shape up.

Mornington did not expect Wick to shape up. Scully was potentially the more dangerous of the two with his eloquence and intelligence; but there would be more trouble from Wicks before the job was over.

Some people were too stupid – or rather, too narrow – to be told.

William examined his book. The corners had been torn off several pages which was the least of the damage; the spine had parted and the book had come in two.

William sighed. It would be a fiddly job, but not too difficult and it would not be pretty. He must beg the carpenter for some fish glue and must sacrifice one of his muslin stocks to join it back together again and reinforce the spine. Still, it was mendable and that meant that Scully could still use it. He shouted for Mr Lord and sent him with a message to Scully and his mess that the book would be back in one piece in a couple of days and they might start studying again.

It was better to send the child than put too much importance on it and single Scully out by going himself.

Scully gathered his erstwhile class about him. He firmly collected those who had deserted in the face of Wick's belligerence as well.

"You heard the Captain" he said "He was obviously in favour of us learning out of a book to make learning the ropes easier for us. So Wick was out of line barging in and trying to make fun of what he's too stupid to manage. Now if Mr Price is able to mend his book and will trust us with it again, that means that he will expect us to defend it against Wick and his ilk. And the captain didn't want any more fighting; so that means that if Wick tries to hurt anyone or fight anyone we ALL gang up and make sure he knows that we stand together and if he tries it on we all bloody well maim him – or throw him overboard. I don't intend to go through this voyage looking over my shoulder for that dancing bear."

Several nodded; and the murmured assent swayed those who would waver.

Mr Lord ran up, almost tripping over.

"Steady son – sir" said Scully, saluting.

"Mr Price's compliments – no I don't give compliments except to the captain or first lieutenant" said little Lord "Mr Price said to assure you that he could mend the book in a couple of days so you might all start studying again and it's an awfully good book because we use it too and I read it on the coach to Portsmouth so I'd have some idea" he came up for air.

"Thank you Mr Lord" said Scully "You hear that boys? We can continue studying."

"Here Scully" a member of another mess slouched up "What about us bein' learned by you too? Why's it exclusive to your mess? Why'd YOU get the book?"

"Because I read fluently" said Scully "And it isn't exclusive it's open to anyone who wants to learn. Only there was problems with Wick and I didn't want my messmates to take a beating. You and anyone as wants to can learn and you have to vow to stick by us and defend the book."

"What about the other watch?" asked the newcomer.

"I could teach them!" piped Mr Lord "Out of my copy! Then the competitions would be fair!"

"That's right nice of you Mr Lord" said Scully "Perhaps we'd better go put it to the sailing master."

Mr Brigham had never had the situation of the two watches being taught out of a book how to handle the ropes; he scratched his head.

"Well I don't deny if you can learn all the names off duty it would be a good idea" he said "Mr Lord, I'll ask the Bosun to stand by to give you a hand, and if I assign each of you a couple of able seamen who can pick up if there's any misunderstandings it might help too. We'll be the trimmest ship in the fleet if you can keep this up!"

He knew that not all the hands would want to bother to study during their four hours off between watches; some would want to take extra sleep, some would not see the point, some, like Wick, would resent the idea. But those who did might yet prove to rate Ordinary Seaman quicker for it – which would enhance their pay to a shilling a day as well as make them more likely to survive. And give the ship a better chance in this mad venture of cutting out a Jonathon ship.

It would not do the youngest young gentleman any harm to have to help the sailors either. Mr Lord was serious enough, but really he needed the bosun to make sure he did not make any mistakes; technically helping young Mr Lord and actually supervising him. However Lord would learn quicker in explaining than merely in learning.

Brigham decided he would put it to the other two young gentlemen when he had them at their navigation classes that if they wished to lend a hand to the lessons he would not be averse.

Which reminded him; he had their noon sights to oversee; and he bellowed for them to come and take their sights and work out the latitude.

Mr Thomas Jenkins might as well earn his two pounds five shillings a month as a full midshipman and the other two strive to be so well paid when they reached thirteen years old and became entitled to the warrant. Colin Prescott was almost of age and Mr Lord looked likely to overtake Prescott if they continued at their usual rate of work.

The boys solemnly sighted with their quadrants and set about scribbling the calculations. Mr Lord's was laid out neatly and was marred only by a small error, which Brigham pointed out; Mr Jenkins might have rather sprawling writing but he had at least a workman like way of doing his calculations and had got the position well within reasonable tolerances; and Brigham sighed over Colin Prescott's.

"Mr Prescott" he said with heavy sarcasm "I hope your calculations are in no wise accurate."

"I beg your pardon?" said Prescott looking confused.

"I believe you will find if you check your calculations that we would appear to be in St Petersburg" said Brigham dryly. "Mr Jenkins, work through it with him if you please; and pray with intense gratitude to the Almighty that even if you boys are prepared to help the green hands to learn knotwork and the names of the parts of the ship and its ropes and sails that at least Mr Prescott will not be required to teach any sailor mathematics. At the moment Mr Prescott your usefulness to the Royal Navy would be better served in handing you over to the French or Americans!"

Prescott grinned, only slightly abashed. He went over it under the tutelage of Jenkins – who did not hesitate to cuff him when his attention drifted – and finally managed an answer not too inaccurate, as the Sailing Master put it when he looked it over, so long as one had a lookout to be sure of not hitting the Channel Islands.

The young gentlemen gratefully escaped and Brigham took their workings to the captain.

"Fit only for the quarter gallery?" asked Mornington. "I heard you trying not to lose your temper."

Brigham grinned at the old joke. The idea that the boys' workings were fit only to use as toilet paper was so often fairly meet. Especially with the more slapdash of the lads.

"Oh Prescott is a heedless scamp who is capable of taking accurate enough sights when he isn't distracted – that wasn't actually his trouble today – and for whom mathematics might as well be written in Hindoo"

Mornington laughed.

"He'll get there" he said.

Mr Jenkins was willing to volunteer his services to help teach the landsmen; he volunteered to help Mr Lord, who might be disappointed now to be only a helper because of having a lordly Midshipman over him, but who was secretly pleased not to bear all that responsibility.

Thomas Jenkins, it may be said, worried too much about making a fool of himself in front of the sardonic eyes of Landsman Scully who was when all was said and done an educated adult even if technically he was well below Jenkins in the hierarchy. Jenkins felt his years seriously and hoped privately that he had not been too cowardly in avoiding the situation by picking the other watch!

Prescott heard the word 'volunteer' and decided that this need not mean him.

"I'm sorry, Mr Price" said Brigham to William "I suggested strongly that they would do themselves no harm in volunteering but Prescott has the attention span of a butterfly on blue ruin."

William laughed.

"A very graphic simile, Mr Brigham" he said. "Even if he were fired with enthusiasm he is the sort of child whose enthusiasm would, I fear, rapidly run thin and abandoning a task half way through is worse than not taking it up in the first place. They will do better without his dubious aid; and for his sake we may hope that he achieves a more serious attitude in the future. As yet he has no need to take responsibility. As he ages; well, time will tell."

"Indeed sir" said Brigham in a voice that did not hold out much hope.

William grinned. He was feeling good about this trip; Wick despite, the novelty of learning from books had seized the hearts of many of the landsmen, and indeed some old hands who were agog to see pictures of what they knew by experience. The carpenter had been helpful with the production of glue and had even helped William put the book back together in a fairly workmanlike job. It seemed to be starting to go very well!

Chapter 6

The captain started competitions of one watch against the other; beginning with sail handling drill. The speed that Scully's pupils gained to earn points was generally wrecked by Wick and his lubberly and unwilling followers – despite being started by the bosun to get them all moving – and the Starboard watch found themselves beaten, just, but the slower but less hampered by truculence, Larboard watch.

The next time Wick came on duty he had a few bruises and was limping slightly. He went about his duties sullenly but at least without visible truculence.

The next competition was won soundly by the Starboard watch and William found himself wondering what threats had been made to get Wick performing with if not efficiency at least not at odds to his fellows.

He noticed Scully, receiving his prize [a quarter of an ounce of tobacco to every man] hand it on to Wick.

"Here, Wick; you did all right; I don't chew or smoke. So thanks for not lousing us up."

Wick took the tobacco looking confused. He was a heavy pipe smoker.

"If you ain't interested in the prize, what for do you care?" he asked.

"Because if we get chased by a bigger ship I want to be able to handle the sails fast enough to run away and live" said Scully "Besides, it's a matter of pride. And I heard a rumour that the officers are putting up a slap up meal at the end of the trip for the watch that wins the most competitions."

If it was a rumour that was all it was; but it would spread now. William went in search of Phrayle. If the men worked hard, not to have their hopes fulfilled would be enough of a disappointment to maybe make some of them bitter.

"Hector, there's a rumour that the officers are providing a slap up meal for the watch that wins the most competitions; will you chip in so it's not a false rumour?"

"Aye lad, I will; it's a good incentive!" said Phrayle "Though I fear me with these orders not all of them will live to eat it. Still, with your bold idea and the Captain's nerve there's a good chance most of them will!"

"The use of French numbers seems to be working well as well" said William "Will the captain explain to the company what's toward?"

"Yes, presently" said Phrayle "No point telling them too soon, lad; that's something you learn by experience. They get overexcited and then lose the edge of that excitement and so make errors when it comes to carry out the plan. The Captain will tell them with about three days in hand to make the ship look more French though the purser's had to give up fabric to make a French tricolour so there'll be a few rumours floating about. Keeping the rumours going at just the right level is an art; and the captain's good at it. By the time he tells them what we'll be doing they'll be ready to throw themselves into the venture."

Scully approached William.

"Please, Sir, there's a rumour that we're to attack France, but we're sailing west; and though that doesn't mean much to a lot of the men, I know that France is to the east."

"Scully, we're sailing under sealed orders and whether I know them or not makes no difference" said William "I can't share anything with the crew. The Captain knows what he's doing and will share what it is in his own good time. You keep up your good work and I shouldn't be surprised if you were rated ordinary seaman by the end of this week and Able Seaman before the end of the trip. Or higher if you care to work at it. If you want to have the worries an officer has, you'd better work hard towards being one."

Scully grinned and saluted; it was a rebuke but a mild one.

"Aye aye sir" he said.

It seemed that Wick had been somewhat subdued by a mix of carrot and stick methods; he did what he had to do and if it looked unlikely that he was going to be rated Ordinary Seaman in any short order he was at least buckling down to the discipline. William thought it was at least partly because he was so surprised at being materially thanked by Scully for pulling his weight that he had half-heartedly given loyalty to a man who could reward as well as organise informal punishment.

Young Thomas Jenkins grinned at William rather ruefully.

"I hear the Starboard watch have an unfair advantage over us" he said.

"How so, Mr Jenkins?" asked William.

"They have three non smokers; and they hold nominations after the competitions they win as to who deserves the baccy most out of the watch" he said.

"A novel way of spurring each other on" said William. "You might suggest that your men each give a finger's length of their baccy and have that doled out as a prize to the best few if they're all smokers."

Jenkins brightened.

"Thank you sir!" he said. "I'll do that!"

William was subsequently cheered by the members of the Larboard watch.

"Please sir" said one of the old hands "We're sorry we thought you might be showing favouritism to the Starboard watch; 't'ain't so, and we see that now."

"I am sorry that you ever thought so" said William. "I loaned my book to a literate man without thought for which watch he was on; but Mr Jenkins and Mr Lord are able to redress the balance. I want both watches to do well. And for your information the idea the Starboard watch had of pooling the tobacco from non smokers was all their own idea."

The man assimilated that concept.

"Reckon we ought to have thought of our own remedy then" he said ruefully. "Main clever man that fellow Scully; now he be pulling in the same direction as the rest of it, reckon he'll be going far" and he grinned. "Reckon a restless so-and-so like that prob'ly deserve it. Ain't for me to hustle that much! Make me fair done to a cow's thumb just t'watch him sometimes!"

William laughed; Scully did have a lot of nervous energy and he quite appreciated that watching him might make a less energetic man a trifle jaded!

The captain timed the evolutions of gunnery drill and the crew waited with baited breath for his result.

"Well now!" said Captain Mornington "I am so pleased to announce that there is no timepiece made that could tell the difference in time between either watch at this competition; and the time was good. I had it in mind to issue bacon and eggs – I have had the cook hoarding the eggs from the hens – to the winning watch but as that won't go round as fried eggs you'll all have to share buttered eggs with bacon. Fortunately I have a good big ham with me so you won't be on short commons with that!"

He was given a rousing cheer. Any change from the tedious diet of salt pork or salt beef and ship's biscuit was welcome; and they had now been at sea long enough for this to be a real prize!

"Deck there! Sail ho!" called the lookout.

"Beat to quarters if you please" said the captain.

The men went willingly to their quarters now, the gun captains no longer despairing of managing to engage any enemy!

The Captain waited looking perfectly relaxed; William envied him that he appeared to have no nerves whatsoever!

Presently the lookout called,

"Deck there! She's a lugger!"

The quarterdeck relaxed somewhat; a lugger was much smaller than a sloop.

"Up the mast, Mr Lord, with the bring-em-near and see if you can make out her colours" said the captain, handing a telescope to Lord.

"Aye sir!" squeaked Lord, his falsetto warble betraying his excitement. This, after all, was his first encounter at sea.

He went up the ratlines, hanging out cheerfully to go round the fighting tops, hardly slowing to be hanging backwards over the sea. It was one of the things William never really got used to as a midshipman, and he was glad as a lieutenant his dignity would permit him to use the lubber's hole instead of going out onto the precarious perch of the ratlines around each yard.

Little Lord solemnly plied his telescope and slid down the ratlines again with what William considered to be more speed than sense; however the child seemed perfectly happy aloft, and saluted the captain.

"Please sir, it's a post office packet sir!" he said. "It's catching us up fast!"

"Excellent" said the Captain "Perhaps there's some news of Boney to be had. Stand the men down from quarters a watch at a time, Mr Price and send them to dinner in turns; pass the word that if there are newspapers they'll be passed down to the crew when the Quarterdeck have had a look. That fellow Scully and the Bosun can read them out for the rest."

"Sir" William did as he was bid. One watch on the guns would be sufficient if this were any ruse; and though it seemed unlikely it was never wise to take risks.

The packet heaved to next to the Thrush and letters and newspapers were brought on board. William had a letter in his sister's handwriting that he thrust inside his jacket to read when he was off duty; he only hoped that it was not news that she was married to Henry Crawford, who had lied so egregiously to her about being able to get William a commission.

The captain glanced at the paper and cupped his hands to his mouth.

"Boney is beat my boys!" he called. "And he is to be exiled to the island of Elba!"

There was a resounding cheer; someone was relaying the news to those below eating and their cheer like an echo almost, joked the captain, lifted the hatches right off!

His reaction to the next piece of news was more of shock.

"Good G-d!" he exclaimed "Lord Cochrane and sundry of his relatives have been indicted for fraud!"

"Good G-d sir!" cried Phrayle "That I cannot believe!"

"Alas, it's all here in black and white!" said Mornington, distressed "He is said to have been part of a fraud circulating rumours of Boney's defeat and death before the defeat at least was reality to get better prices to sell shares on the stock market; dear me, it centres round the sale of Government bonds of more than a *million pounds*! It says…. 'Lord Cochrane, a radical member of Parliament and well-known naval hero, his uncle the Hon. Andrew Cochrane-Johnstone, and Richard Butt, Lord Cochrane's financial advisor were implicated. One Captain Random de Berenger, who had posed both as Colonel du Bourg who had announced Emperor Napoleon's death and as one of the supposed French officers telling this faradiddle, was soon arrested, and a guilty verdict was returned against all three charged in the case.' Dear me, a year in gaol, a thousand pound fine and an hour in the pillory, Lord Cochrane stripped of his Naval Rank and expelled from the order of the Bath!"

"Well sir he could always volunteer and enlist with us" said Yarde, the Cox'n, who had the wheel.

"Damn your eyes for an impudent bastard Yarde" said Mornington.

"Aye sir" said Yarde.

"Yarde, you may pass the word about, that the man who has done most for trying to reduce flogging and increase pay in the navy is now alas a gaolbird like half of them and so will enter even more into their feelings" said Mornington. "The implications of course are that they have lost for a year at least one of their most outspoken allies. WHAT a foolish thing to do!"

"I suppose sir, even rear admirals as clever as Lord Cochrane are not immune to foolishness" said Phrayle. "Though a thousand pound fine when they have gained so much is fairly derisory!"

"We don't know what he wanted the money for" said Mornington "He's a great man and a good one; it may have been for a hospital for sailors invalided out for all we know. But it was wrong to do it; I am disappointed in him."

"Sir, might it be that he left his own Government Bonds in the care of a relative or this financial advisor while at sea and he is innocent and has merely had his name used?" asked William.

Mornington stared.

"It may very well be!" he said. "Cochrane is a canny seaman and a cunning warrior but somehow I find it hard to see him as a fraudster!"

Yarde was heard to mutter something about a *ruse de guerre* against the Tories.

"Yarde if I have another word out of you on the subject you'll be on a charge" said Mornington sternly.

Yarde saluted.

He knew the limits had been reached at which he could presume on his captain's good nature no longer.

Whether Cochrane was knowingly guilty or not he neither knew nor cared; but he was as dismayed as the officers that the seamen's champion had been caught at wrongdoing.

It was news that the more intelligent men would find an unsettling piece of information to offset the news that Boney was defeated and sent into exile.

Chapter 7

William read the letter from his sister Fanny – it was crossed and crossed again so it took some deciphering – that declared in glowing terms that she had accepted an offer from Edmund Bertram who was not after all going to marry Henry Crawford's sister Mary.

William was glad. The Crawfords were a frivolous pair and not in the least like their uncle, his patron, Admiral Crawford, whose private life might leave much to be desired but who was a good officer. Of course, from the point of view of anyone marrying into his family, a scandalous situation such as the Admiral's open removal of his mistress to his own home with his dead wife barely cold in her grave might be an impediment. But the Admiral had taught William much and gave him the confidence he needed to face the board of examiners with enough calm to do well enough to pass for lieutenant.

Admiral Crawford would be much upset by the news of Cochrane too; they had much in common in their care for the ordinary sailor. Well, there was nothing that might be done about it save to carry on, as the Captain would, along the principles laid down by Cochrane of strict discipline without harshness.

William sat down to write a reply to Fanny, expressing his best wishes; if a letter was ready written it could go if they had another fleeting encounter with a packet boat that was homeward bound.

He wrote that he was enjoying his promotion, pondered over writing any details and deciding against it. Fanny was a good girl but she would not understand most of what he wrote! Nor in all likelihood would Susan; ah, that was what Fanny had written, that Susan was to go to their Aunt and Uncle Bertram as a companion in her stead when she was married to Edmund. Susan would fulfil the position very well; and probably more merrily than rather staid Fanny, the penalty, he supposed, for being the eldest sister. Like being a more senior officer.   Alas for their sister Mary, who had died; she entered into his hopes and aspirations and would have enjoyed a letter full of naval life. William sighed, and laughed. Perhaps Betsey would grow out of being spoilt and would become interested. He wrote another letter to Susan, penning some incidents he hoped would make her laugh in case she was interested; and then wrote a third to the rest of the family. That was his duty done to his family for the time being; and now it was time to try to hammer some geometry into the minds of those pesky boys in the hopes that one day they might recall enough to use it.

He would use the incident of the Diamond Rock to explain using the thrilling story of how Commodore Sir Samuel Hood had swayed guns up the sheer cliff of the rock off Martinique to dominate the channel there.

It was an exciting tale that any boy should be stirred by; and he could ease some very important principles of mathematics and seamanship into it.

"I swear there's a mutinous assembly going on" said Brigham in the wardroom. "You might trust that fellow Scully, Mr Price, but there's been angry voices and he's been the centre of it."

"I don't think he'd start any mutinous assembly," said William, "if there's anger I expect it's some misunderstanding that can be easily redressed or he's been arguing against mutinous assembly. I'll have Lord bring him up here and we'll ask him."

"Your protégé certainly works hard enough" said Phrayle. "Here, I'm senior here; I'll send Lord."

He put his head out of the Wardroom door to bellow the boy's name.

Lord turned up fairly quickly.

"Puh-please sir, it wasn't me!" he said in a squeak.

"What, did you think you were in trouble?" asked Phrayle "I will do if you look any guiltier. Hah, you know that trouble has been perpetrated and you are afraid of being blamed; don't worry, when I find what the trouble is I know better than to blame anyone but Prescott. You're here to nip below decks and fetch up Scully."

"Aye sir!" said Lord and charged off.

"Has anyone ever noticed," said Phrayle, "that boys have two gaits – fast asleep and gallop."

The others chuckled.

"It's to do with them growing" said Campbell. "Half the time they need to sleep to catch up with it and the other half they're exercising to stretch their legs."

"What's a knowledgeable man like you without any vices I can see doing going to sea?" asked Phrayle, idly.

"Well it's this way," said Campbell, "when I was a boy I wanted to join the navy; but my father was adamant that I should study medicine. He had his way of course. When I qualified I put in a year learning surgery as well helping in the Greenwich hospital for sick sailors; I've a small legacy from an uncle that allows me to be independent so rather than buying a profitable practice I could afford to do *pro bono* work. But having learned how to amputate and such matters I decided that I would combine my boyhood ambition with my training and applied to the navy which pays me to do very little between battles especially with so liberal a captain that treating flogged backs is a duty conspicuous by its absence I am glad to say."

He broke off as Lord returned to announce Scully.

"Thank you Mr Lord" said Phrayle. Lord darted off back to whatever activity he had been interrupted at. Phrayle regarded Scully. "Scully," he said, "you'd not be part of any mutinous assembly, would you?"

"Nossir" said Scully. "I have too much to lose now. I have ambition."

"Would you then tell me why you and others have been meeting and becoming angered?" asked Phrayle.

"Oh sir! That's not *mutinous* sir" said Scully "We were angry about Lord Cochrane being done down; some of the hands as know more say it's a scurrilous lie designed by the Tories to keep him out of doing good for the sailors. We were wondering how to approach the captain to say we'd put our names to any document he wished to put together protesting our belief in his innocence."

"Well I never!" said Phrayle. "A Petition! Price, you organise it; the Captain may not set his name to any such document but I will; and any seaman who can sign or wishes to make his mark will be right welcome and if the Government don't like it, I make no doubt that Cocky himself will be right touched. Admiral Crawford will see it forwarded to anyone who should see it. Well done Scully; and behind these doors and never in public, Mr Brigham and I apologise for doubting your intentions."

"Aye" said Brigham "I know when a man tells the truth."

Scully saluted.

"Thank you sirs" he said. "I know the nineteenth article!" he grinned "And it doesn't cover seeing some joke laid for someone who might deserve it" he added.

"Oh Dear G-d WHAT has Prescott done now?" groaned Brigham. "Don't answer that Scully; it wasn't a question unless ratting on him is going to get him out of worse trouble for being caught doing it."

"I should think he'll get a good caning sir" said Scully "At least I heard him say it was what he anticipated; so if he's expecting it and thinks it fair exchange, then he knows what he's about."

"Thank you Scully" said Phrayle. The man fit too well into the wardroom; discipline had to be maintained. "The explanation is perfectly satisfactory; you may pass the word that Mr Price will be round with a declaration that he will read out to the effect of the belief of the company in Lord Cochrane's innocence."

"Yes sir; and that's all we can sign to sir" said Scully "Because expressing an opinion without demands isn't mutiny. That's one of the things we were discussing, legal wording of it."

"Ah, yes, you have legal knowledge; excellent!" said Phrayle. "Carry on!"

Scully left and William went to get paper and a pen to draft up a document.

"Well Hector, it shows one thing" he said "That the company have become a crew; that they are ready to work together to show indignation on the part of someone else."

"Yes by George, you're right!" said Phrayle.

Prescott was duly caned for having left in the gunner's cabin a rat dressed in a facsimile of the gunner's uniform in a makeshift cage. He professed it well worth it to have managed to see the gunner's face when he caught sight of the rat. Especially as his rat had bitten the gunner when the cage was opened.

"If you put half as much effort into your work as you do into elaborate larks you would be a model sailor" grumbled Brigham as he groaned over the boy's noon sight. "How can a boy who can make a perfect miniature uniform that almost fits a blasted rodent manage to take a sight that puts us off Martinique?"

Prescott decided that discretion was the better part of valour and looked docile while Brigham shouted at him. He knew he had been a bit slapdash taking the sighting.

Standing at certain angles was a little painful even if less so than sitting down. One paid; and the payment had been largely for the surgeon's first customer of the trip with the gunner's thumb.

William had not been amused that his friend Campbell had needed to do such work; rat bites could be nasty and the gunner needed his thumb. Evidently Prescott had forgotten everything William had said to him at the beginning of the voyage. Prescott found the boys' officer somewhat cold during their lessons with William.

"It was only a joke, sir!" he protested.

"A fine joke which might have cost a conscientious man his livelihood if we had a less competent surgeon to see that the thumb doesn't fester" said William. "A gunner needs his thumb. You've forgotten all I told you about consequences. Next prank you play, the wardroom won't see you caned; we'll prank you back and see how you like it. And I guarantee you, Mr Prescott, since I have three younger brothers, *my* imagination is considerably greater than yours."

Prescott flushed beet red; his face was a study!

"I'm sorry sir" he said.

"Don't be sorry to me" said William "Go and apologise to Mr Porkins. I don't suppose you meant your blasted rat to bite him and forgot what it could mean in your delight that it did. You've accepted punishment so he'll know it isn't an attempt to wriggle out; I think you'll find it means a lot to him."

Prescott nodded and went off to do William's bidding; little nuisance as he could be, he did not lack courage.

Once he had stumbled through the apology and explained that he had never thought about the rat biting or that a gunner needed his thumbs, the dour Porkins was quite mollified and proceeded to explain that if Mr Prescott thought that he enjoyed punishing boys when he had two at home just a little younger he was wrong but that failing to perform the right actions with a dangerous thing like a cannon meant death either for the idiot who had been stupid, or all too often some other poor devil who happened to be in the way.

Prescott had never thought of this either and promised to take better notice in future.

The incident was perhaps for the best in the long run; and when Porkins reported to the wardroom, William had him in stitches over the description of the horror on Prescott's face at the idea of being pranked back rather than being caned!

With the signing of the petition – and almost the whole ship's company wanted to put their mark beside their name, inscribed by William – there was really a good atmosphere among the crew.

There was one flogging; an old hand had horded his tot and got roaring drunk. Like Prescott, he knew and accepted the consequences of his action and accepted it as fair.

Mornington was angry; he hated being forced to flog any man.

"Peters," he said, "do you know why I have to flog you?"

"Because I horded my tot and got drunk sir" said Peters.

"Yes; but why should that be a flogging offence?" asked Mornington.

"Because it always has been sir" said Peters. He thought hard. "Was it because of what I called the members of the Admiralty?"

"No though it didn't endear me to you that the young gentlemen learned words and er, vices like that" said Mornington. "The reason that drunkenness is a flogging offence – and mark this well, my boys because it's important – is because a man who is drunk can do stupid things. Singing a scurrilous song about the Lords of the Admiralty and a number of Covent Garden, er, ladies is relatively harmless. Deciding to undo the knot that bends the vang to the deck eyelet because it might be funny to see it wave about could kill someone. Or suppose he couldn't get to his post in time because he's stupid with drink and that means we lose a spar in a gale? A man who is drunk can kill himself and his comrades. THAT'S why I'm flogging you, Peters; for putting your mates at risk."

"I see sir; no capting ain't never explained it to me before," said Peters, "so I ain't never thought about not doin' it agin. I won't never do it agin, sir, honest; havin' yer fun and takin' what's due for it, that's one thing, but if I'm likely to endanger me mates, that's another. You'll think I've turned Methodee."

"Good man" said Mornington. "If you stick to that you might manage to make it to able seaman too; according to your record you've come close several times and lost the credit for being punished. An extra sixpence a day has to be a good incentive as well."

Peters brightened.

"Aye sir" he agreed.

William hated watching the punishment; but Everett the bosun got it over with in a fast and workmanlike manner and Peters was not bleeding as heavily as some flogged men William had seen. Peters' messmates helped him below where Campbell was ready with salt to put on the cuts to help fight infection.

The mood of the crew was however good; you could always tell if they thought punishment was fair or not and there was nothing of the brooding heavy silence that indicated disapproval. They moved back to their duties and were quickly laughing again over some witticism one of them cracked. And Peters himself bore no ill will.

Chapter 8

The manoeuvres and training continued; the Captain put up half a guinea apiece for the watch who might win a competition of night time sail handling without a command being given out loud. There was some puzzlement over the reason behind these evolutions, but Scully thought he knew why.

"See here, mates" said Scully to his disciples "The Captain has something in mind for night work; and we're going to win those half guineas. And the sixpence out of each ten-and-six into a pot same as the tobacco."

Peters, who was on the Starboard watch and had started to join the extra work nodded.

"And that work he has in mind seems likely to be with a French flag. And them numbers we works to that you say is French. But I thought Boney was defeated?"

Scully nodded.

"That's so. But I think I know where we're headed – where a French ship would be neutral. And that's why we're handling the courses with French numbers. In an American port, any word of English is going to be understood; and will kill us all. We're going to cut out a ship those damned Yankees have taken as a prize I reckon!"

There were gasps at that.

"Bit bold innit?" said Wick

"Audacious is the word you want, Wick" said Scully "But fortune favours the bold!"

"D'you fink he can do it?" asked Wick.

"Yes" said Scully firmly.

"I've sailed with the capting before" volunteered one of the old hands, a man named Hartley. "What he sets out to do, 'e does; and 'e does what 'e can to minimise risk to 'is men too. 'E'll do it all right. Or rarver, we'll do it for 'im" he said. "We're bloody good now; fanks to you new 'ands bucklin' dahn ter work, and there'll be prize money in it, you mark my words!"

The night manoeuvres went well.

Starboard watch won – they were determined not to be left out of any action that might be in the offing – but Larboard watch did well too.

"I can see I'm going to pledge all my prize money for this trip!" laughed Captain Mornington "Larboard watch did so well there's five bob to each of you too. But Starboard watch have won the privilege of becoming a prize crew and you shall know more in a day or two."

"If you please sir," called Scully, "we reckon we know."

"Well Scully, perhaps you'll tell me what you think" said the Captain.

Scully outlined his thoughts.

Mornington nodded.

"You're not far out, Scully" he said. "Not spot on the nail, but not far out. And from now on, all the sail handling is going to be done with French numbers called only; so you all get in the swing of it. And any French speakers see Mr Price who will organise you into standing around idly discussing the relative merits of French and American whores and liquor."

There was laughter.

William grinned. His French was improving with lessons from Scully after the boys took their lessons. Scully would certainly be one of those chatting nonchalantly about whether the Americans understood either venery or viticulture.

And being Scully he would appreciate the use of alliteration in the English of that for the words were likely to be in his vocabulary.

The officers clustered around a map in the captain's cabin. It depicted part of the eastern seaboard of America, with rivers and settlements and forts, and the arrangement of offshore islands that being parallel to the coast looked as though they should have been part of the land but had been isolated by the sea invading the land behind them.

"It's an old chart," said Mornington apologetically, "it dates to 1781 when New London was sacked and burned under the leadership of Benedict Arnold."

"I can never figure out in my own mind if he's a heroic patriot or a miserable traitor to his own" said Campbell.

"Oh at the time maybe he considered himself a British Patriot putting down a bunch of rebels" said Phrayle.

"I hate to disabuse you, Hector," said Mornington, "but he was a general in the rebel army first and changed sides. In my book a man who can change sides once can do it again; if it had been up to me I'd not have trusted him. However, he seems to have served the British cause faithfully even if he was a treacherous dog to his erstwhile friends. And we cannot know the circumstances that caused him to defect his services to America; perhaps he himself felt betrayed in some respect. However, what he did do was to bring knowledge of the firing arcs of the forts on the River Thames – and yes, they do say it like that to rhyme with James."

"Mind you, some of those who fancy themselves as society are so mincing-mouthed that they pronounce James as 'Jems' to rhyme with Thames" laughed Phrayle.

"Odd types, the Americans," said William, "they don't have the originality to call their towns by anything except new – name of English town – nor their rivers it seems; and then can't even pronounce them properly."

"Well half the Pilgrim Fathers were from Norfolk and Lincolnshire and the like and I have yet to hear that they've spoken English there for centuries" quipped Phrayle. With action in the offing he was in a particularly good mood, looking forward to making fools of the Americans.

They concentrated on the area of the chart that showed a river opening just north of the long island that made blockading the town of New York so easy. There was an island called Fisher Island protecting the coast from the Atlantic swell; and Mornington tapped his finger on the town of New London.

"The reason for the sacking of the place in 1781 is the same reason we're going to take it as a target now" he said "It has always been an anchorage for privateers, some of whom are little better than pirates. This island, Fisher's Island, gives then the opportunity to sail close hauled up the coast behind it and elude the blockading force. Our main blockades are on the city of Washinton and further south but be aware we might have to explain our presence to British blockade ships. However, in case of American eyes, I would rather try to outrun them."

"Why would they chase us now just because we wear French colours though sir?" asked William. "The war is over; France is at peace with England."

Mornington gave him a look of affectionate exasperation.

"Will, we were fortunate to be overhauled by a mail packet. She might, or might not have been carrying despatches for the blockaders at New York. If she was not, they may not yet know that Boney is beat. So they may perceive us as the enemy. However that is a fact to worry about only if it arises. Note we have a small problem – well two main potential problems."

"Aye sir; Forts Trumball and Griswold" said William. "They command the channel very well."

"Fort Trumball was burned out by its own men, who also spiked their own cannon, for being in an untenable position with a limited garrison" said Mornington "We have to assume a new fort was built. Fort Griswold is formidable; an oblong as you can see with the longest front to the river and bastions at two opposite corners;

according to information I have the walls are some ten or twelve feet high at the lowest with projecting stakes and built of stone with ditches to protect them too. There are embrasures for small arms fire as well as the cannon on the platform. We would do better not to be fired upon by such a fort; even assuming that Fort Trumball has not been rebuilt to even better specifications."

"What is this third fort in the town?" asked William.

"I believe it is a firing platform for small arms," said Mornington, "so there we have the disposition of the fort; there is anchorage from well before the forts that extends past them, all covered by the guns. Any questions?"

"Wouldn't it be easier to scuttle the 'Thrush' ourselves sir?" said Brigham with rather heavy gallows humour.

William was excited.

"You don't expect the forts to fire at all sir, do you?" he said "That's why we've been practising silent night sail handling; we pick a likely ship to cut out, swarm over her and take her and sail her out under cover of darkness without anyone being aware that she has been taken."

"That's the idea" said Mornington. "I confess I've half a thought to send our marines and some volunteers to take Fort Trumball if it's not so formidable as Fort Griswold hoping to take them by surprise – bringing a gift of French wines, say, and overpowering those who open to us. But without knowing anything about it that's a venture that may be too risky so I would rather not engage upon it unless they seem alert and suspicious. We will be looking for a privateer which has given most of its crew liberty; which is to say, most of the crew ashore and drunk. And no, Will, you won't be swarming over her – not in the sense of fighting that you were thinking of. You'll deal with the deck watch only and batten the others down below. Not forgetting to lock the captain's cabin and closing off all the hatches to the wardroom as well as to the lower deck. We'll rendezvous at sea to open up and take those left aboard as prisoners. Otherwise the risk of the noise of fighting is too great."

William nodded.

His heart was hammering; did this mean that *he* was to be in charge of the cutting out? The captain had said 'you'.

Hector also thought so.

"Excuse me sir, will not I be leading the cutting out party?" he said in some disappointment.

"No Hector" said the captain. "Mr Price is expendable."

"He's also clever and imaginative and came up with the initial idea" said Phrayle "You are right sir; my apologies for a momentary jealousy" and he nodded to William and managed a tight, but genuine, smile.

"Hector you are the most generous man alive!" said William warmly.

Hector Phrayle clapped him on the shoulder.

"I'm a good first officer, lad; but I do know my limitations. And I'd be a fool not to see that the man who has the ideas is the man who should be in command of the prize when we cut her out."

"Which being so, pest as he is, I'd like Prescott with me as he thought first of using French colours" said William "I'm glad Starboard watch won the right to take the ship; Scully is the cleverest of the men aboard and his own bunch will understand the need for silence."

"What of Wick?" asked Brigham, concerned.

"I think Scully has virtually tamed him," said William, "showing that there are potential rewards as well as punishments. Besides as he is a man who'll act for enlightened self interest, once he has it pointed out that there may be prize money in the offing, a decent schooner-sloop will not do the men any harm if it is condemned as a prize even if it is not so rich a prize to take as an enemy merchantman. And even with a depleted crew, whoever we batten down below will count towards head money."

"That's the truth" said Brigham, much relieved. Young Mr Price, he reflected, had the mood of the men well and Scully had proved more an asset than might ever have been guessed at first! "Where am I to be, sir?" Brigham asked the captain.

"With Mr Price on the prize" said Mornington. "Hector can do your job adequately. Moreover the sails will be different and the men will trust you to understand them."

"Permission to suggest to Scully that he and his men study schooner rigging?" said William.

Mornington hesitated.

"Granted" he said "Not that we know quite what manner of ship we shall hope to take until we get there. We may even stay a few days deciding what our prey may be; which will be a strain not to speak any English but better than picking a ship that looks innocuous and it turns out to be transporting troops."

The other officers felt cold at the very thought!

Scully took the advice to look at other types of sails like schooner rigging with a nod and a thoughtful look.

"Aye sir" he said. "Am I to infer that we are not perhaps sure what the rig is of any ship we may be called upon to sail?"

"You might very well infer that though I doubt I'm supposed to comment" said William.

Scully gave him one of his shy grins.

"If I may say so, sir, now my hands have stopped hurting, I believe I'm enjoying myself more than I did as a clerk," he said, "at least with this little puzzle to solve. There's a lot to learn it's true, but there's a beautiful logic to the way the sails work, and I have to say I find the mathematics of that more to my taste than the mere adding of columns of figures."

"I think I should hate being a clerk and cooped up in an office over dusty old ledgers" said William frankly. "It was a career my mother would have liked me to pursue for its safe shore based nature; but my father was a sailor and the sea is in my blood. And for a clever man there's a lot of opportunity to be found – though less chance of promotion with a nasty outbreak of peace against France."

"Do you think sir that Bonaparte is going to remain tamely on Elba?" asked Scully.

"I shouldn't think so" said William. "The better for us to make a good showing in this venture and get the plum jobs when he starts to roar again."

Scully laughed.

"I would never have thought of myself as one of the death-or-glory boys," he said "but the prospect of outwitting the Jonathons is certainly exhilarating. And there is a lot more of interest at sea than in conveyancing and copying wills. And though it might be improper to wish for hostilities to break out again against France, well, it does mean more chance of promotion; am I wrong to consider that?"

"Well as I feel the same exhilaration – and could never even raise a mild interest for clerk work – I quite enter into your feelings" said William. "You probably don't know, but one of the toasts in the wardroom is 'A long war and a sickly station', rather a black piece of humour in hoping that deaths of more senior officers mean more rapid promotion."

"I see, sir" said Scully. "So the seaman's prayer that the roundshot be distributed in equal proportion to the prize money, the greater part on the quarterdeck, is a prayer shared by junior officers?"

William laughed.

"In principle – though in practice I'd hate anything to happen to my fellow officers" he said. "How well are your hands adapting?" he recalled the comment that Scully had made.

"Not too badly at all sir; though as one of those with softer hands and no calluses from any hard manual work I have noticed it a lot" said Scully. It was an honest assessment delivered with a shrug, and no moan.

"I understand Mr Campbell has a patent ointment for blisters with a hardening agent in it?" said William.

"Yes sir – I mean Aye sir" said Scully "And it's very effective. The new hands are all very grateful to him for it for none of us were used to handling rope at all."

"I'll pass that on," said William, "he'll be most pleased."

Chapter 9

The captain mustered the ship's company and explained that they were temporarily, and for the purposes of a ruse, about to become French.

"Ooo la la!" called one wag.

"Indeed," said Mornington, "and a word of English could kill the lot of us so carry on with ooh la la if it's all the French you can manage but if any Yankee sailors look at you oddly put your backs to the walls me lads."

There was much laughter.

Mornington let them enjoy their joke then spoke seriously about what was required of the company and how they would being off an audacious theft without, hopefully being caught at it.

"Free cheers fer the capting, wot's a bowman prigger o' vessels!" shouted one of the newer members of the crew.

"Have you any idea what that meant, anyone?" asked the captain of his officers as the company cheered.

"Not a clue sir" said Phrayle.

"Hrm, I fancy a 'prigger' is a thief" said Brigham "And I believe 'bowman' is to be good at something."

"One lives and learns" murmured Mornington "One might guess if they would but stick to cant nobody would ever recognise it as English. Very good; Mr Brigham, carry on in converting the ship to being French."

The carpenter had already been asked to carve boards to fit over the name to be 'La Grive' which translation meant that the lively figurehead would not need to be changed. William said doubtfully that he wondered if it should be 'La Grive Musicienne' to be songthrush; but as the captain said, the English did not require that made clear so why should the French especially when this carried more risk of the carpenter making a suspicious misspelling.

William agreed!

The ship had originally been 'La Merle', the blackbird; but this had unpleasant connotations in English since blackbirders were slave traders, and the figurehead had been repainted with the name change. Moreover it was possible that the Jonathons might have discovered that 'La Merle' had been captured; and accordingly become suspicious. A new name was safer as well as not requiring disfiguring the brown, speckled-breasted figurehead with black paint.

Brigham had enthusiastic helpers from the ship's company meanwhile making the ship more French; they were deployed, according to the dry language of the log 'As the Service Required' usually shortened to ATSR. So unimaginative an acronym did not begin to cover the dirtying of a deck that the crew worked so hard to holystone to a pristine whiteness, throwing around plenty of 'slush', the dripping skimmed from cooking the salt pork and beef, and rubbing the deck not with holystones but with cloves of garlic to induce the characteristic smell of a French warship. Scully, whose French was educated, began to sing,

"*Quelle est cette odeur agreable…..*"

"If you fink it's agreeable you're deaf in ve nose mate" said Peters.

"It's a French Christmas carol" said Scully.

"We learned it at school" squeaked Mr Lord "And it always puzzled me that anyone should think shepherds should smell agreeable at all."

"Oh, it isn't that, begging your pardon, Mr Lord" said Scully "*Quelle est cette odeur agreable, bergers, qui ravit tous nos sens* has a comma or two in it; it translates as 'Oh, you shepherds, what is that pleasant smell which assails our senses' because the *bergers*, the shepherds are implied as being 'O shepherds' like your vocative case in Latin."

"Oh I *see*!" said Lord. "Thank you Scully; now it make a *lot* more sense."

"You're welcome, sir" said Scully.

"Gawd, I'm glad I ain't a gentleman" said Peters. "'Ere, Scully, mate, you orta be a bleedin' orficer."

Scully looked enigmatic.

There were three other members of the crew who could manage some French; one was the servant of an émigré who had been unable to afford to keep up his household and who had been taken up by the pressgang; one was an ex French prisoner of war who had volunteered rather than rot in the hulks because as he said all governments were *'sales cochons'* and one might as well die one way as another but in the air was preferable; and the third had been a prisoner of the French and had picked up enough to seduce the women of the garrison where he had been held. His nickname was not repeatable on the quarterdeck. It did however carry a degree of respect in the idiom of the coarse sailorman.

The émigré rejoiced under the name of Napoleon because he had been notable for a degree of arrogance when he had first been pressed – he was one of the old hands now – and the other Frenchman went by the name of 'Haybean' because he was wont to start most sentences 'eh bien' which had been duly mangled by the crew.

They, Scully and the officers were to provide most of the conversation; and some the officers would of course dress in slops to make their relative positions more ambiguous.

Napoleon had done his best to make uniforms more uniform in the French navy and the egalitarianism of the republic was eroded by a need to have properly trained officers. However as Captain Mornington said, it was fortunately unlikely that the inhabitants of New London would know any more details than they did and so long as in general they wore dark blue, doubtless they would get away with it. Providing dark blue jackets and trousers for all the company did not best please the purser, nor a scrap of red so each man might seem to have a scarlet waistcoat too; but Mornington said cheerfully that at least he was not called upon to use his own blood to dye the red.

"Well, Capting, the crew'll be right happy to wear scarlet weskits" said Yarde the Cox'n "The more red baize we has on us, the less floggings there can be for want of red baize bags for the cat."

"Yarde, you're an impudent son of a gun" said Mornington.

"Aye sir" said Yarde.

Mornington laughed.

"Mr Price," he said, "having a cox who isn't afraid to speak up is an invaluable thing for any captain; and I should be failing in my duty to train you if I did not tell you so. At the risk of swelling his head so much it won't go through the hatch, I consider Yarde to be indispensable. I can be inclined to brood and his unfailing good humour – and frequently terrible jokes – help me to keep things in perspective. A good cox can apprise his captain of the mood of the crew without needing to say a word; and can manage a judicious and non prejudicial sniff if his captain proposes doing anything stupid. I don't believe Yarde has yet had to sniff at me" he added. "He can also be a go-between to the crew by dropping judicious hints if there is any shall we say misunderstanding. I'll advise you to temporarily rate Scully as your cox although he isn't yet rated able seaman because he has that capacity. Now I never said any of this in Yarde's hearing or to you and he's still an impudent son of a gun."

"Aye sir" said William.

"Aye sir" said Yarde.

William also realised that Yarde could joke about the red baize because he knew that floggings *would* be few and far between; and that too told that the mood of the crew was lighthearted. When the crew larked about and made jokes it was the sign of a happy company – and a happy company was an efficient company that pulled well together.

It was also a good sign that there had only been one application to change mess; seamen might mess with whom they chose, and could request a change each month. Frequent changes of mess spoke of discontent and trouble within the company. The 'Thrush' had small messes of eight men; some ships had as many as a dozen messing together, sharing cooking utensils and a trestle to eat on. The mess areas were spotless too – William had been on inspection only a few days before – with the eating and serving utensils shiny clean, and neatly arranged in the cutlery rack or hung on nails. This air of domesticity also augured well for the way the men worked together.

Haybean was enthusiastically teaching a group of men a song he knew to learn by rote; Scully raised his eyebrows a few times, shrugged, and helped them with their pronunciation. William did not know half the words in it and decided that in this respect he was probably the happier.

"Please, Mr Price, what is the song about?" asked little Mr Lord.

"Mr Lord, if I knew, I suspect that if I told you I should face something far worse than court martial" said William.

"What's that sir?" said Lord, balancing on one leg.

"Your mother, in righteous anger" said William.

"Do you mean it's *smutty*?" queried the child.

"Somehow, Mr Lord, I believe it goes so far past smutty that the bosun would be shocked" opined William. "And *no* Mr Lord, you are *not* to learn the words to it in the hopes of finding out what it means later."

"Nossir" said Lord who had been considering it. Still, he thought, hearing it over and over as others learned it, nobody could really take issue with him if he learned it accidentally. Such casuistry pleased him so well that he performed his allotted duties for the rest of the day with such aplomb and dispatch that it must be said that Brigham wondered if he were sickening for something.

It was a good exercise; singing French songs would make the sailors feel that they were really a part of the venture and any French speakers in earshot would hopefully run a mile to avoid hearing the lyrics in too much detail without taking account of the fact that the adventures of a little priest sent to sea were being bawled out in a mixture of English regional accents from Peters' broad Essex speech to the tones of Yorkshire from one of the older hands.

"Wot abaht Scully's carol wiv sex in it?" demanded Peters.

"Sex? It has nothing to do with sex!" said Scully, outraged.

"Yes it do" insisted Peters "I 'eard yer, 'sex hile something' you sang."

Scully sighed.

"*S'exhale t'il rien de semblable*" he said "Is nothing to do with sex, it's that you leave a part of a word out because of the way it's pronounced; "It breathes – exhales, the word is similar – like nothing else is what it means. Anyway it isn't Christmas" he added firmly.

"Eh bien, mon ami, what can one do?" said Haybean. "There are those determined to 'ear English words in amongst the French just because some words are similar."

"Why are they similar?" asked Peters.

"Because when France was Gaul it was conquered by the Romans as Britain was and we both get words from Latin" said Scully in exasperation.

"Oh, the Romans! That'll explain it" said Peters. "Was that before or after Enery the fiff beat seven bells aht of the Froggies at Ajincort?"

"Long before" said Scully.

"Well that'll explain it" said Scully.

What it explained was a mystery to Scully; but at least the slow thinking but good natured Peters was satisfied.

"Romans; thems the ones wiv Julius Caesar" said Wick. "There's a play about him. He gets stabbed" he added pleased to show off his erudition to Scully.

"Indeed he does" said Scully "Wick is quite right."

"See? I ain't as stupid as some on yer thinks" said Wick.

Scully decided that this was probably a good last word on the subject and hastened to suggest a last look at schooner rigging before taking a couple of hours sleep.

The ship was soon as unshipshape as Brigham could manage without actually crying; there were even frayed rope ends hanging down in places.

"It's not that the French are poor sailors so much as that they have been badly led" said Mornington by way of explanation in front of Yarde, knowing that the cox would relay his words. "The revolution killed off most of their officers who understood *why* certain things are done to make things shipshape as well as *how* to do them. This led to perfectly adequate seamen being in charge but men who did not understand the reasons for keeping the ship as clean and tidy as possible. And when the men saw it as a waste of time and were likely to declare anyone who cared to be to fancy an aristo it was actually dangerous to be to nice about such things. So being slipshod was a habit that became general. And over the years this was so normal that nobody questioned it. With the little Corsican things began to tighten up – and seamen had a uniform of their own too – and seamanship in theory became as important as in practice for officers and things began to change. But it's easy to drift into slipshod ways; smartening up a whole navy and changing the habit of a whole generation or more of sailors is not so easy, especially when those sent to make changes have only the vaguest idea what is required. Any British officer could smarten a French ship's crew because of knowing what is required."

"Being blockaded can't have helped morale either sir" said William "Won't that have a poor effect on smartness?"

"Yes indeed, Mr Price it will do," said Mornington, "and sitting around idle also becomes a habit that it is hard to shake – as well, as you so rightly point out, as the feeling of despondency of there being little point in trying. I hope that we strike the right balance here of being seamanlike enough but with some rather mucky ingrained habits."

"I think a few loose ends of junk roughly coiled might add too" said William thoughtfully "Moreover sharpened cutlasses could be hidden under such coils of rope. And boarding nets."

Mornington nodded.

"A good detail my lad" he said. "Very well; see to it!"

"Aye sir!" William saluted and set about making sure of extra piles of junk, old rope, as concealment for other things. It was good to be able to add to a plan with his own ideas!

Chapter 10

The French Tricolour was bent on as soon as the ship came close to the American coast; and Mornington's and Brigham's joint navigation was seen to very accurate.

The ship appeared to be heading directly for the coast; but soon it became apparent that an island would be passed to port with a wide channel of about two miles between it and the coast.

"Stand by to come about" said Mornington.

Brigham nodded.

"*Oui*" he managed.

"*Eh bien, ça c'est bon*" said Mornington.

They would use French from now on; voices carried over water. Brigham called out the string of orders in French numbers that would see the ship turn to port into the sound between island and mainland; presently they would wear into the river and would beat up it. Mornington was pleased; it might take time to tack up river but it meant that so long as the wind remained steady it would be behind them to get away. Of course this would favour any schooner-rigged ships of the Americans; but with luck they would be away before there was any pursuit.

It felt odd, William thought, to see land on both quarters; at a goodly distance it was true, but still an almost stifling feeling. Or perhaps that was fear over what was to come. He *was* frightened; and it was no point denying it. However all he could do was his duty to the best of his ability; and not let the fear control his actions. He hummed '*Ça Ira*' to give himself some courage.

"Cuh, Mr Price be a right cool hand" muttered Wick to Scully up on the main yard.

"He's paid to be" said Scully dryly.

Scully did NOT like heights; if he glanced down some little devil in his brain seemed to whisper to him to jump. He knew this was a bad idea and concentrated on not looking down. If he pretended the spar he was on was just a wall he was just fine.

Wick had insufficient imagination to be scared – of anything. Scully sympathised with William and had a shrewd idea that the young officer was whistling purely to keep his courage up. High above the deck there was a better view; and as the River Thames came into view, Scully's new found understanding of the tactics he had been reading about made him aware that it was a very tight place to be in indeed.

Well if he wanted to be an officer some day he must deal with the knowledge and the fears an officer must also deal with as well as just taking orders for now. They had come across the wind that was in the northwest to turn into the roads here – he knew now that a sound between an island and the shore that was navigable was a road – and would wear, or go into the wind to go upriver. And even sailing close hauled they would not get up it without some extensive tacking, going backwards and forwards, going forward a bit at a time to get every scrap of wind that they were going – no, he corrected himself, beating – against. Well getting out should be easy; pity it was also as easy for the damned Yankees. At least being fore and aft rigged meant that beating up the channel was easier than if they were fully square rigged; and gave them manoeuvrability. Scully now knew what the vang was for and could appreciate the subtleties of the rear mast's configuration. He could also appreciate what William had meant about having the fore and aft rig on the mizzen being more effective; it stood to reason that it was easier to turn the ship with pressure nearer to the ends than the middle, even as one might use a finger to turn a log floating in a pond.

William climbed the ratlines and nodded to the seamen as he settled into the tops with a telescope.

"We'll be coming out under darkness" he said "And somehow I don't think that yon lighthouse is going to be working while we are at war; and I'd as soon not put our prize on the rocks. Do you lads mark well the position of all rocks and promontories too. Scully, you'll be my cox; I rely on your memory of rocks and shoals to help steer a way out."

"Aye aye sir" said Scully, smartly, pleased that he would have a position of responsibility. He had taken more than one turn at the wheel because he did not get flustered by a rapid series of orders concerning direction change. "Sir, Peters is good with the lead; should he be forrard to sound the bottom?" he hoped he did not sound self conscious about saying 'forrard' in the naval fashion.

William considered.

"I'd like to agree but we'll need an experienced topsman like him to sail the ship" he said. "If we were overburdened by crew I should say yes. However, no reason Mr Prescott shouldn't do it" he added. It would keep the lad out of the way and too give him a responsible job that hopefully would make him rise to the occasion.

"Aye sir" said Scully dubiously.

William grinned.

"Mr Prescott won't learn any younger or under less pressure" he said. "And with a man in the chains, even if he is not as accurate as Peters, we shall be no worse off than having nobody there. And I know what you're thinking, all you lads and I'm not about to condone anyone saying it out loud."

There were some rueful grins from the topsmen; the thought that it could be worse if Prescott reported deep enough water and made a mistake so they ran onto a shoal had crossed most minds. But Mr Price was right; the same might happen if they had no leadsman.

The harbour was busy; and a small boat came out to meet them. It was a small schooner, some kind of coast guard vessel.

'La Grive' was duly hailed – it was pronounced to rhyme with 'dive' – and Captain Mornington greeted the hailers cordially in French.

They were called upon to heave to; with hand signals to make it plain. Having hove to the small boat came up to them and an officer scrambled up the accommodation ladder as it was let down for him.

"You parley any anglais Moosoo?" he demanded.

"Mais oui, citoyen" said Mornington, enjoying himself "We 'ave coom to your port wiz ze wines and to reprovieesion. But you 'ave not 'ailed us by name; pourquoi pas?"

"Yes I did" said the officer "La Griyve"

"Ah! I deed not understand you' mispronunciation" said Mornington. "It is 'La Grive, say GrEEV for me and you will be doing parfaitment, n'est-ce-pas?"

"When I want a damned schoolmaster in some outlandish lingo I'll hire one" said the officer truculently. "As if it ain't enough with the ruddy Dutch! I don't need none o' your sauce, Moosoo! You have any trouble with the damned English?"

"Non, zay 'ave not trouble' us at all" said Mornington. The fellow seemed convinced even with a slightly forced French accent; of course his own native accent left nothing to be desired in terms of educated pronunciation and idiom, even taking the American accent into account. *Not* a gentleman this officer judging by his flattened vowels and poor grammar. Possibly that was why he was commanding a coast guard vessel. But then the Americans were republican like the French though at least they did not seem to have taken their republicanism to the extremes the French did. But it did mean that one might meet with persons who were not gentlemen even in positions of responsibility.

Mornington was the son of a small landowner and not by any stretch of the imagination as high born as many officers; but he was unquestionably of gentle stock and impeccable if bucolic lineage. He welcomed the concept of those who wished to better themselves, such as the Gunner, who spent every last penny he had on putting his sons through his local grammar school so that if his sons went to sea they might do so as midshipmen not ship's boys; and Scully was plainly well educated and his rise was quite in order. But Mornington had his prejudices and they included those people whose accents betrayed them as what he considered low considering themselves to be in any wise his social equal.

He did not, however, betray this mild contempt for the American; and told himself that if the man was a half decent seaman doubtless so new a country had to take what it could get on smaller vessels.

And as to the Privateers, well all such persons were low, whatever nation they hailed from; and he was glad that Britain at least was strict about the issue and if necessary the revoking of letters of marque.

He listened to instructions of where to dock and noted to himself where the instructions might easily be misinterpreted if he felt like it. That opened up a lot of opportunities to be exploited.

To be too compliant could be suspicious; everyone knew the French were slipshod and did things in a lazy fashion. Indeed he noted the disgusted look the officer gave to the grease on the deck and the way he walked fastidiously to avoid the chickens that had been permitted out to run about. In fact the man, pulling faces at the stink of garlic, made himself scarce as soon as he might.

"*Abiit, excessit evasit erupit.....*" muttered young Mr Jenkins.

Mornington cuffed him, though not hard. It was an international rebuke as might be understood in any language for an excess of Latin and an insufficiency of caution.

There were times and places for Cicero and this was not one of them.

"*Abies erupis* yourself, cub, up the mast, and remember all you see" muttered the captain, believing – correctly – that Mr Jenkins' French would not have been equal to following the order if he did not risk relaying it in English. Jenkins looked startled for a moment then was off up the ratlines. To anyone watching he had made some comment that had been unacceptable, had been cuffed and then also mastheaded, a common minor punishment for midshipmen in any man's navy, since as well as being uncomfortable to spend a couple of watches aloft, missing a meal into the bargain, it placed the offending youth out of the temptation to cuff him silly.

Napoleon the émigré was at the wheel so that Mornington was able to pass orders in shouted French; and Napoleon was grinning broadly at the careful misunderstandings that his captain was passing on. Any French speaker would have to admit that the misunderstandings were not really unreasonable and were quite logical. Judging by the disbelieving consternation on the face of the American officer – William had a surreptitious glance through the telescope – he knew no French and could hardly believe his eyes that the French captain should be so stupid.

The coast guard vessel drew close and the American officer shouted a lot and waved his arms to emphasise his disapprobation.

Mornington smiled and waved cheerfully as he headed right up the river past the forts as though he did not understand the opprobrium in the shouted oaths and vituperations. Mr Lord was out of sight behind the bulwarks writing down new curse words.

The American was jumping up and down and threw his hat on the deck in exasperation as the vessel drew alongside the 'Thrush'.

"Whare in tarnation do you think you are going, Froggie?" he demanded.

"Eh bien, I go where you tell me, citoyen!" called Morninton happily.

"No you damn well are not!" howled the unfortunate American.

"What is it zat you say? First you say go 'ere, now you say do not go 'ere? I wish you will make up your mind!" cried Mornington feigning irritation. Napoleon chose to go about at this moment allowing for a confusion in the sail handling orchestrated by the old hands who knew how to make a ship look badly sailed; and for a moment there was a very real danger of sinking the coast guard vessel if it did not sheer off. They proceeded even further up river by this device while Mornington shouted at his citizen helmsman for making his own qualified decisions and Napoleon stormed that he was but following standard orders. There was quite a lot to be seen while this pantomime was played out. Also a lot to be smelled; and there were disgusted noises as the smell of the whalers in the port assaulted the nostrils.

There were manoeuvres to bring the coast guard alongside again; and the American officer came distastefully on board.

This time he drew a sketch map of where he wanted Mornington to anchor; which being down river of the forts was a less nervous place to be.

Mornington threw a fit of Gallic exasperation and shouted at Napoleon to wear ship and bring her round..

They had had the opportunity however to have seen all the harbour; and to see all the shipping in there.

And to note that the small and rakish ships likely to be privateers seemed to favour the anchorages down river of the forts. Which would make life easier.

Mornington followed his instructions this time; and at a hiss from William aloft the sails were furled far more clumsily than the crew had learned to do by now and the ship drifted vaguely into the anchorage with a level of seamanship that almost broke Brigham's heart to see.

The crew found it highly amusing. Scully indeed was almost weeping with laughter from the whole exercise and was glad to be aloft out of sight of the Americans. He was alive to how dangerous it might be to be seen to be laughing and hissed a warning to his fellows too. It was good that the crew was relaxed – but there was such a thing as too relaxed. But it had worked – they had come, they had seen, and that made it more likely that they would conquer, he told himself, if one might mangle Caesar a little.

Chapter 11

The town of New London was substantially new, mostly having needed to be rebuilt after the burning of it some thirty three years previously. Though the board faced buildings were weathering to a greyish colour, bright golden wood showed that new building was going on as well. Some buildings were painted white; some were built of a brown stone, especially those on the rise that seemed to designate the centre of town. Scully kicked some of the men for staring and pointing at the unfamiliar Mansard roofs on some of the buildings, since they were also known as French roofs for good reason and should not be, he hissed in an undertone, a cause for supposed Frenchmen to gape like a hayseed in the metropolis.

Napoleon was sent ashore with Scully and Haybean and Higgs, the seaman who had been a prisoner of war in France; they were armed with lists of provisions and the intent of not buying anything. Napoleon was looking forward to it; he knew he could be quite uncertain about any goods and would need to return to check with his captain. It took up time; and gave them the opportunity to look round town and determine which of the privateers seemed to have sent their crews on liberty.

They discussed in French that Captain Mornington was a captain of the greatest, since most captains would have sent an officer with them, even if it was only a midshipman, because they had only to beg for asylum and escape the navy if they chose; and to show such trust in them argued a great spirit. Loyalty to such a man meant that none of the four would dream of deserting even though only Haybean had actually volunteered initially. Higgs reckoned that the life was as good as any, Napoleon had an easy life being captain's servant most of the time and Scully had his ambitions as well as his loyalties. They did take advantage of the liberty to sample the local liquor and Scully discovered that he disliked the local spruce beer even more than he disliked the rum issued daily by the pint since they had moved out of home waters where beer was issued by the gallon. However a foray into drinking establishments meant the chance to overhear loose talk. Especially once Haybean had sung his song – with actions – for an appreciative audience, doing a good impression of being several sheets in the wind as Higgs described it. Scully filed that description of being drunk away in his memory, and was pleased to realise that this phrase referred to a situation with the ropes not properly adjusted for the wind, as would leave the sails uncontrolled and flogging, and the ship as unsteady as a drunkard.

They reported back to the captain and officers that two of the schooner-sloops had crews at liberty; the Mosquito and the Rapier. The skylight was closed so they might converse in English in low voices.

"And by the gossip, the captain of the Mosquito is being hauled over the coals by the governor and he and his lieutenants are facing an enquiry over a supposed mistake in capturing a merchantman that was actually American" said Scully "Which a mistake it might be but speculation in the town is that Captain Henry Burkett has succumbed to the temptation to turn pirate. His men were allowed to leave before all this sprang up this morning and most of them are dead drunk. I think it's the best bet; anyone still aboard can't be anything but despondent I should think."

"Unless they are raging pirates at heart" said Mornington "But they must be demoralised at the least; what about the Rapier though?"

"The Rapier is an older ship, less weatherly" said Napoleon. "And we were not sure if it was a general liberty or watch-by-watch."

Mornington nodded.

"The Mosquito sounds likeliest" he said. "Did you find out where she's moored?"

Scully grinned.

"Just on the other side of the pier to us sir; fortune favours the bold and all that."

"Quite so Scully; I'm glad you steered clear of Latin, I've had enough of that from Mr Jenkins" said Mornington.

"Well sir, the young gentlemen do like you to know that they are working hard" said Scully indulgently.

"There are times and places however for showing off" said Mornington dryly. "Very well; those of you in the Starboard watch take a watch below; you need to be fresh. Pass the word that the Larboard watch is to rest also mess by mess. Well done you men."

They saluted and left.

William was feeling almost sick with excitement and no little apprehension; but he too made himself take some rest. Though both ships would sail out of port together, the hands of the 'Thrush' at least knew her sails well enough and would not have to be alert for any problems arising from unfamiliar rigging.

At least now they could examine the rigging of the Mosquito and see in advance what if anything might cause a problem; and William bored himself to sleep repeating the names of every rope from memory.

The Mosquito was a two masted ship both fore-and-aft rigged; schooner rigged with a foremast and mainmast. All the cordage and sails looked to be in good condition and the lines were rakish and promised a good turn of speed. She appeared to have twelve guns and a long nine-pounder bowchaser. That marked her as an aggressor; she expected to come up behind an enemy with that heavy sting not in the tail but in the head. A broadside of six guns was nothing to a ship of the line but to a merchantman probably carrying a total of four guns it was formidable enough. She was not quite as heavily armed as 'Thrush' in terms of the weight of the guns but she was certainly more manoeuvrable; it would be a bold man who would wager on the outcome of a fight between them, assuming captains of equal prowess.

Indeed, it would be the seamanship that would determine the outcome if it came to that, thought William, strolling up on deck after a refreshing sleep to glance apparently idly at the ship that he hoped in just a few hours would be his prize.   He noted a guard at the companionway to the great cabin. Perhaps the captain was being held below on the orders of the governor pending a court martial or whatever the Americans did; or maybe he had pirate treasure and set a guard of his own men to watch over it. William suppressed a grin. The words 'pirate treasure' were enough to get the heart thumping in excitement; what a silly boy he could be at times! Still it would explain a guard.

He wandered over to Wick who was also stretching out after a sleep; the big man found the hammocks very cramping.

"Wick" said William, hardly moving his mouth "You're a good shot with a belaying pin" he recalled that Wick had been gauntleted for throwing a belaying pin with unerring accuracy to strike the mast having changed his mind at the last moment and had NOT thrown it at Everett the bosun.

"I been keepin' me temper in check sir" said Wick, managing to mumble "I don't want ter be hanged" he added with honesty.

"You've done well" said William. Wick looked surprised but pleased. William went on, "Glance over to the ship across to port. Reckon as you could hit the sentry on the head with the knob of a belaying pin from here?"

Wick looked.

"I'd do it better from on the quay" he said. "Clear o' the riggin' see."

"Then tonight I'll be giving you the word to do just that" said William.

Wick looked pleased.

He opened his mouth to bellow 'Aye Aye sir' but William reached up to put a hand on his mouth.

"Sorry sir" muttered Wick.

"I too for the discourtesy of touching your face; no rebuke was intended just a warning" said William, aware that it could be interpreted as a blow to the face, which whilst a seaman would have to take it from an officer, was an insult.

Wick grinned at him conspiratorially and tapped his nose, winked, and nodded his head towards the blissfully unaware sentry and mimed sleeping.

This was almost worse than speaking out loud, but William dared not risk more conversation; he clapped Wick familiarly on the shoulder and turned away.

Darkness did not come until late in the summer night; and they waited too until the pale sliver of the waxing moon had set, a couple of hours after midnight.

Then before doing anything else, Captain Mornington punctiliously hauled down the French colours and raised the union flag, and had the false name boards brought inboard; an act of audacity but one that was unlikely to be noticed. It was however a point of law that he and his officers could swear to be fighting under their own colours when it came to actually taking an enemy ship; such was the way ruse de guerre worked.

Clad in their dark clothes the sailors of the Starboard watch assembled on the deck of the 'Thrush' and William gave the nod to Wick. The big man ran with surprisingly light steps from the bulwarks down the boarding plank to the quay and with a flick of the wrist the belaying pin was gone.

William watched, heart in mouth, as it somersaulted through the air; in a perfectly judged trajectory. There was a heavy THUNK and the guard pitched over onto his face, his gun clattering as it hit the deck.

Scully sprang forward over the bulwarks to cross the quay and leap on board the other ship; and jammed the sentry's hat onto his own head and picked up the musket; anyone glancing over would see the guard where he should be.

He should have waited for orders; but it was a good thought.

Wick stood waiting to be told what to do next. William beckoned to his contingent of men and they surged silently across the quay, a moving shadow within the darkness. William signalled to drop as a hatch opened; and they followed him in dropping to the ground.

"'Sup?" said a sleepy voice, addressing the sentry.

"Nut'n" said Scully, hoping he had the idiom right in copying the voices he had heard.

"Right" said the owner of the voice. "You better not get any funny ideas 'bout the captain's cargo 's'all joe."

Scully grunted; and the hatch closed again. The silent surge of seamen resumed, William himself securing that particular hatch with wedges. The seamen below would hear the mallets driving the wedges home but there would be little they could do with all being secured simultaneously; and William relied on their initial horror and likelihood of running to the companionways to try to force the hatches, hoping there was not one who had the ability of lateral thinking to slip through the hawse hole and swim to give the alarm.

The guns were all on the upper deck here; including the bow-chaser, so there would be no portholes to suggest easy egress. On the 'Thrush', the two stern chasers were in the after cabins, the first and second lieutenant's cabins, on either side of the great cabin.

William used the one in his cabin to hang his clothes on while he was dressing.

He was effectively captain here though; at least for the time being. He walked aft to Scully.

"Good work" he said quietly "Some would have called it insubordination; you need to judge your officer."

"Thank you sir" said Scully. "Peters has fastened the great cabin door by tying it up."

"Good work" said William. "Pass the word.... Oh, Peters, you're here; tie the skylight down as well please"

The flash of Peters' teeth in the darkness and a hasty salute showed that one of the men at least took the idea of silence seriously. There had been one low oath, but generally the whole operation was so far conducted very well. William nodded to the waiting men and pointed aloft. They took to the ratlines in a silent hurry as though choreographed; and William thought it a more skilful and a prettier display of grace and athleticism than anything that might be displayed at Covent Garden or even any of the vaunted displays of acrobatics at Astley's Amphitheatre.

What the men of the British Navy did every day, often in foul weather and a howling gale, was scarcely less impressive than the feats of the highwire walkers in their safe circus ring under cover.

Which in reality made it the more impressive. Save that the public paid to see the feats at Astley's and in general despised the jack tars who kept the nation safe from seaborne aggression.

"They're a bloody good bunch, Scully and you can pass that along" said William quietly. "Ready?"

"Aye sir" said Scully. William waved at the men on the capstan; they must join the others aloft almost as soon as the anchor was aweigh to make sure there were enough hands to the sails.

The capstan turned, without the usual accompaniment of music to put heart into the seamen working it; and William felt way on the ship as she moved beneath his feet. He beckoned to Prescott to help him bring the anchor the rest of the way inboard, and dismissed the sailors with a wave of his hand. He and Prescott strained on the weight of the anchor, feeling it increase as it came clear of the supporting water; then one of the ship's boys ran forward to 'nip' the rope to hold it inboard, giving the name of 'nippers' to small boys.

The ship creaked, sounding happy to be preparing to go again to sea; and the sails flogged briefly as an insufficiency of men loosed them.

They were under way; and truncated triangles of the big courses and the inverted triangles of the gaffs unfurled and caught the wind.

Chapter 12

Passage down the big river was swift and silent; William glanced back and almost gasped; there was a ship quite close behind them. Then he thought scorn on his own fears, for it was none other but the 'Thrush' running before the wind as they were, with all canvas set to make as speedy a getaway as possible. It was a glorious night for it, the stars sharp and bright in an almost clear sky, just the slightest wisps of cloud that heralded more wind to come. The stars looked close enough to touch!

They were running away from the 'Thrush'; William looked back, assessing as they came round a slight curve in the river, that 'Thrush' was very slightly down by her head; a dozen cannonballs taken aft would probably be enough to cure her of it but she wallowed and griped by just the slightest amount; enough to knock a knot or two off her sailing speed.

He was pleased to have noticed it, and told Scully to tie the wheel and collect Mr Prescott to take a look as the boy had a while in hand before he would be needed as a leadsman.

He pointed it out to both of them.

"So even a er, well-found ship well sailed can need trimming, sir?" asked Scully.

"Yes indeed; and I'm hoping that someone on the Thrush has watched our progress to see if we need trimming too" said William. "By stowing provisions or cannon balls in a different place a lot of difference can be made; but you must not overdo it" he laughed "When I was the same age as Mr Lord and not much younger than you, Mr Prescott, I went out in Portsmouth harbour with a friend – we had a small fishing smack that two boys could handle – and we were down by the head. We were silly and over-enthusiastic and we moved everything we could to the stern and almost capsized ourselves. My friend's father, who was watching, said we almost had the keel out of the water. You can have too much of a good thing."

"Thank you sir; I'll remember that, sir" said Prescott. Whether he would or not might be debateable; but he had some good instincts, and William fancied that the boy would be more likely to recall a story told against himself by an officer than some laudable but impersonal example. He was excited about having a vital job in the chains making soundings; and William was glad he had given the boy a responsible job. William dismissed him back forrard with a nod and resumed his stance on the quarterdeck, feeling the loneliness of command really for the first time.

"Beg pardon, sir" said Scully "But I fancy we want to come up a couple of points to starboard to avoid what looked to me like shoals on the way in and it's a bit much to expect the men to deal with, without warning."

"That much?" said William, startled "Not that I'm doubting you Scully."

"I believe the wind's come over a point or two and it's busy trying to blow us onto the sandbank" said Scully sounding worried.

William beckoned to the ship's boy.

"Tom" he said, hoping he had remembered the child's name correctly "Up aloft with you and tell the men on both masts that well be coming round a couple of points to starboard – yes, I *did* say starboard – and then they must watch for my signal to swing round to port as we clear the river mouth"

"Aye-aye sir!" squeaked the child and scuttled up the ratlines.

Scully watched him.

"And at that, sir, it's a better life than being indentured to a chimney sweep" he said.

"You were reading my thoughts about children at sea, Scully" said William. "I was thinking about my little brothers who I'd not like to see as ship's boys or powder monkeys. But it is at least a better life than climbing chimneys, half stifled with the soot, growing up deformed as I understand, those few that even survive to grow up. Or toiling in the mills, running in amongst dangerous clashing machinery to clean blockages, maybe losing a limb. Well they might lose a limb at sea but at least there's usually a surgeon on board – even if our surgeon here that Mr Campbell can spare used to be a horse doctor."

"And still better than no surgeon at all" said Scully. "Life at sea can be cruel hard but for the poorest I don't say but that it's kinder than some of the lives to be had on shore. At least, with a decent captain and good officers. That wasn't meant as toad-eating, sir."

"No Scully, I know; we have the privilege here of being able to speak man to man with a reduction in the constraints of discipline" said William. "I confess I've not had time to consider the plights of the indentured foundlings; I've been a part of the blockade against slavers and so have worried about their plight; especially in trying to come to terms with the fact that my Uncle owns a plantation in Jamaica and therefore must own slaves. For though the traffic is banned, slaves are still owned; and I believe any born into slavery are still slaves. I have seen the poor people crammed into slaving ships so close together they suffocate, some of them; to maximise the cargo. And though they look so different, Scully, they are still people, frightened people; I have seen a woman, released from chains by our men, pet her children in the same way my mother would do to little Betsey, with the same look of fear and wariness in her eyes my mother would wear. It is evil."

"It's these Americans that do most of the slaving now, isn't it?" said Scully.

"Yes; it is" said William "But we cannot be free of the taint ourselves until the slaves on Jamaica are free, or else we are hypocrites. Perhaps however it will have ceased by the time you or I rise high enough to do anything about it; but it makes me consider entering Parliament one day if I might do so – and too to carry on Cochrane's radical work."

"I'd vote for you sir, if I had the property qualifications to do so" said Scully.

William grinned.

"Well this ship will be condemned as a prize for a goodly sum" he said "At least a thousand pounds; maybe more. And also it depends what cargo she's carrying if any, if she has taken any materiel from a merchantman and it hasn't been unloaded. Which if it's truly an American ship that was plundered means that we may get to keep the sale price in prize money. If there's British goods plundered it will be returned, that's the rule. The men who know that will be hoping that he really did act the pirate against his own. As I suspect he may have done or there would be much crowing about taking a British ship as would have scotched the rumours."

"Dear G-d, sir, have we possible slaves battened down there?" asked Scully in shock.

"No Scully; once you've smelled a slaver you never mistake it" said William "It's awful; far worse than the whalers upriver some of the lads were pulling faces over. It's more likely to be cotton; but let's not take cargo into account. Even with the ship alone that's five hundred pounds between the crew and the lower warrant officers, four eighths. That's near ten pounds apiece for you all."

"That's eight month's wages for a landsman" said Scully. "And more than half a year for an Ordinary Seaman."

"A better proportion than for me" laughed William "My share of the eighth to the officers would be twenty five pounds – about two months pay. Well I shall be able to replace my uniform with it."

"And we still have to get the ship home to sell sir" reminded Scully.

"Quite right, cox" said William. "That was finely steered; I could hear breakers on a bar as we passed the shoal. Mr Prescott has not sung out any warning however so I fancy either we are in a good channel or he has become mesmerised looking for mermaids. And I didn't say that about a young gentleman, Scully."

"Didn't hear a thing sir" said Scully. "Is the 'Thrush' following our track?"

William glanced aft.

"They are" he said "Captain Mornington pays us – you really – a fine compliment in that."

Scully looked pleased.

"We're about to go hard to port soon sir" he commented.

"She handles well" said William.

"Yes sir; very responsive to the wheel" said Scully "Almost skittish; and I wonder if she might be a little too trimmed down by the – er aft end."

"Stern" said William "You've picked it up so quickly I sometimes forget that you've not long been at sea."

"Thank you sir" said Scully. "It is more exhilarating than an office, once one knows the ropes. Though I have indulged in a little whimsy" he said.

"I'll indulge it further and hear it" said William.

"I had a vision of barristers in their wigs, stood on the dais in court as though it were a quarterdeck, ordering clerks to load escritoires with powder and firing ledgers at the opposition" said Scully.

William laughed, stifling it with his hand for too hearty a laugh would carry too far.

"A delightful whimsy" he said. "Can you draw, Scully?"

"No sir" said Scully.

"A pity; for with a few changes to represent the Lords of the Admiralty and their clerks it would have made an excellent satirical cartoon that I fancy the Naval Gazette or the Review might have printed and paid you for" said William. "Ah....." they came out into the swell of the ocean, broken somewhat by the island offshore but still with a bit of chop to it. William waved a hand to the men aloft; Scully swung the wheel; and they were coming round, out of the river and into the roads with the wind on the port quarter. The sails were swung to accommodate their change of direction and soon filled again after the briefest of times limp.

William did not signal the men down from aloft until they had cleared the island and must deal with adjusting the sails to account for the ocean's full vigour as well as the wind; then he put his fingers in his mouth and whistled a creditable imitation of the bosun's call for down from aloft.

The men came scrambling down in co-ordinated chaos; they were more visible than they had been going up and the stars were paler.

"Quarters me lads" said William; it being the Royal Navy custom to greet the dawn at quarters.

"Please sir" a lugubrious seaman said "Powder's below."

"DAMN" said William "Of course it is. Go to quarters anyway lads; it's good practice to be in the right place. If we come under attack we must act the nervous virgin and hide behind the 'Thrush's' skirts. Or is that wings?"

The men laughed good naturedly and went to their stations as the sky on the starboard bow lightened and became stained with the myriad colours of dawn.

"There's green in it" said Scully, awed. "I've not had time to look much at sunrise and sunset before; it's worth being at sea for this."

"It is one of the better moments" agreed William. He beckoned the midshipman over. "Mr Prescott; take the bring-em-near and keep a watch out for any signals from the 'Thrush'; presently Captain Mornington will call on us to heave to."

"Aye sir!" said Prescott, taking the telescope and scampering up to the first fighting top.

The sky continued to lighten.

Peters came up and saluted.

"You can see a grey goose at a mile" he reported.

"Very good" said William "The men can stand down; there'll be no breakfast until we have the prisoners secured but they may go mess by mess to the scuttlebutt for a drink."

"Aye aye sir" said Peters.

The men were grateful for a refreshing drink of water; the spray aloft left the taste of salt in the mouth. William had a drink himself and relieved Scully to take one too when Prescott slithered down.

"The message says '1362 and 873, heave to'" he said self importantly "'139 Captain 118 boarding 388 immediately'"

William took a quick glance and surreptitiously checked Prescott's translation. He had got that all right any way.

"Very good; acknowledge if you please, Mr Prescott" he said.

One of the seamen had already bent the flags of acknowledgement on for Prescott who pulled on the halyard to send the bright flags fluttering into the sky.

A couple of boats put out from the 'Thrush'; and William noted that one was full of marines, just in case of trouble. A sensible precaution. He stood by to welcome the captain on board; and sent Prescott aloft as look out just in case there was pursuit, and too to keep him out of the way.

Prescott was quite capable of peering down a hatch and tumbling down to become a hostage.

And then the boats were at the side of the ship and Captain Mornington was coming up the accommodation ladder.

"Well done my boy" he said. "Fortune indeed favours the bold as your cox said. Let's get this business of sorting out prisoners over with quickly so we can both be under way with no chance of being caught up with."

Chapter 13

The first hatch was opened and William gave the order to come up with hands in the air and surrender. There was some muttering below and half a dozen or so sailors came up the companion way with their hands raised. They were tied up and stowed beside the now fully conscious and angry sentry.

"It was a foul move" he said "Those damned limeys had false colours!"

"Which were struck and substituted by our own before we even left our ship" said William "If you had been at all observant you might have seen; or at least heard the screech of the halyards."

"Aw nuts" said the sentry "I didn't take no notice of it; there's allus squeakin' blocks an' such on ships."

"That's what we rather hoped would be the attitude of most" said William.

The redcoats meanwhile were passing through the lower deck checking that all the seamen and supernumeries on board had been taken; and called it to be clear.

"Do you mind if I send a cooking party below to start breakfast, sir?" asked William of Captain Mornington.

"Not at all lad" said Mornington. "I could do with my own – one we're under way again."

William gave the orders; and a redcoat came up to report.

"All clear below sirs" he said "And a cargo stowed of tobacco and coffee; look like there's been some seamen from the Yankee ship broke into it already" he reported.

Which being so William had no doubt that a little more had vanished into the pouches of the marines inspecting for their own use, or to pass on or sell; but he was not about to say anything. If he brought it to official notice the punishments for peculation were draconian; and to mention it in front of Captain Mornington was to bring it unavoidably to official notice.

The cargo was still technically the property of the owner from whom it had been taken, and until or unless condemned as a just prize by the prize courts breaking the cargo was theft and any thief subject to punishment accordingly. And then of course it was theft from the ship's company. The sailors knew this of course; and if it were shared around fairly they would keep quiet, taking the fact that the Jonathons had already broken the cargo as fortuitous. Well, William had no desire to see men hanged for a momentary temptation – that he could not *know* had taken place anyway.

Mornington was looking to William to make a decision.

"Very good" said William "Have someone who can draw make a sketch of the state of the cargo where it has suffered peculation; Scully!"

Scully came over.

"Sir?"

"I need you to be acting purser and accompany a man who will draw the extent of peculation and sign it as a true account to go in the log; and so see to having it re-sealed to the best of your ability. I'll have a guard on the cargo at all times; stealing from our own prize is stealing from the prize money of all hands" he raised his voice so that it carried.

Stealing from the cargo if they could get away with it, and thus in their minds the government, would not be seen as so much of a crime by most of the men; making it clear that the cargo counted as their prize would make all the difference.

Tobacco and coffee might not make it a treasure ship but it could increase the value of the prize by a considerable amount; indeed it was the cargos that made taking prizes valuable, even if it were likely that so handy a little ship should fetch some reasonable sum herself.

"All right, what were you guarding in the Great Cabin?" William demanded of the sentry. The man scowled.

"Why should I tell you, limey?" he said.

"Aw, he's going to look and find out anyhows" said another of the American sailors "Watch out, Limey; it's a dame and she's a right virago; anyone would think she had rights as a human 'stead o' bein' a mulatto girl."

"You mean that captain of yours kidnapped a girl?" William was shocked

"She ain't a girl; she's a black" said his informant.

"Any more of that disrespect and you go over the side" said William grimly. He strode aft, and untied the knots holding the skylight down.

"I beg your pardon ma'am" he called "I had no idea there was a lady on board as a prisoner; I'm coming down to release you right away"

"And about time too" said a female voice.

It sounded as educated as any voice of American intonation might be expected to be.

William went to the great cabin door and undid the Gordian knot Peters had set on it and opened it.

He gasped.

The young lady was beautiful!

Her skin was a soft café-au-lait colour with eyes like chocolate and tumbled curls of a rich chestnut cut in the latest of styles. She wore a modest round gown of figured cream muslin, over an apricot satin petticoat, high necked and with one modest flounce and trimmed with ribbons of the same apricot as shimmered through the sheer fabric; and though William knew little about fashion he was fairly sure it was modelled after some Parisian design and was of the first stare.

He made a bow.

"Your servant" he said "Lieutenant William Price of His Majesty's Sloop of War 'Thrush' and Acting Captain of the prize 'Mosquito'."

"A long title for a young man" said the lady, dropping a beautiful curtsey "Amelia Finch; daughter of Amos Finch, Merchant; *legitimate* daughter."

William blinked.

"Er, would there be any reason to think otherwise Miss Finch?" he asked.

She gave a bitter little laugh.

"You English are so quaint!" she said "My mother was a mulatto woman as you must see in my face and features; and though she was freed and my father married her under English law on Jamaica – she was Jamaican – I am a prize of war and a possession to Captain Henry Burkett. I suppose you have not killed him?" she asked hopefully.

"Alas, Miss Finch, I have not yet had that opportunity" said William.

Miss Finch coloured prettily.

"What I pray you is my status?" she asked.

"Damned if I know" said William frankly "Well, not a prisoner anyhow; I mean, one doesn't keep ladies as prisoners. Only you *are* American and the enemy so I ought to keep you under observation or something" he added uncertainly.

She gave him a sideways look.

"Will that be a hardship?" she said.

"Errhhrm" said William, flushing in embarrassment. She was far too easy on the eye! "Far from it and that's not good. I would ask that you remain strictly to the quarterdeck when promenading; I don't think any of my lads would offer you insult but let's not put the temptation of a beautiful lady anywhere near them. Um..... do you happen to know how come this Burkett turned pirate?"

"Oh yes" said Miss Finch "It was because of me; which in a gothic novel would be flattering but in real life is really most unpleasant. He.... He had lewd designs upon me and asked my father to sell me; which led to my father striking him since I am free. He swore he would possess me – and I did not like the way he looked at me. So my father determined to send me to France to a finishing school for a year for my own safety. The ship I was on was the one that Burkett decided to take; one of father's own merchantmen with a cargo bound for Nantes. That filthy pirate killed all the crew so they could not tell tales of him and my virtue is only intact because I wounded him with a hair pin and hit him over the head with the cabin's Utensil."

"I see" said William a little shocked at such forthright disclosures. Evidently American ladies were less coy than English ones "That sounds remarkably enterprising. When we left he was being held by the governor of New London on suspicion of piracy."

"Well I hope they hang him" said Miss Finch.

"I fear without your testimony they may have trouble bringing it home to him" said William "As we have also stolen the evidence in terms of the cargo. Dear me! Well as you are half Jamaican and therefore British I think the safest thing for now is to take you to Britain rather than to France, although we are now at peace with France; Bonaparte is defeated."

"Well that will be good for trade" said Miss Finch. "At least French merchantmen will be able to cross the Atlantic unhindered. Where however would I go in England? The enemy?"

"Dear me" said William "I do not think my mother.... She.... My family is not very wealthy. Nor very well educated or.....cosmopolitan. Perhaps Admiral Crawford and his wife will offer you a home; because they are childless and he is the patron of both my Captain and myself" he brightened. "And you will not be seen as the enemy if you only say that your mother is Jamaican."

"I guess that would be suitable" said Miss Finch dubiously. At least this young British officer seemed to mean well; and besides though the sound had not travelled well through the skylight, the use of Henry Burkett's speaking trumpet applied to the ear had enabled her to overhear much of a conversation with a man called Scully that had revealed much about this young man that was not displeasing. "How may I let my father know that I am safe?" she asked.

William pondered.

"Write a letter to him outlining all that has occurred and if we come upon a French packet, a neutral ship, it might be carried on that" he suggested.

She nodded and her glorious curls bobbed enthusiastically.

"Thank you Mr Price" she said.

"Er, have you an abigail?" he asked.

"No" said Miss Finch "I was to engage a French maid when I reached France; I am not helpless."

"Well.... If you retain the use of the Great Cabin you can lock the door at night" said William. "Excuse me; I have a ship to sail."

He hurried off; it was time to get under way.

He sent the men aloft to unfurl the sails then sent them to breakfast, with a few maintaining their positions brought food by Tom the cabin boy.

He also had food sent to Miss Finch; the sentries had taken the prisoners to the 'Thrush' and they would be fed there.

He knew full well that the sailors would have added up that seven prisoners meant thirty five pounds head money and would be arguing whether Miss Finch counted for a five pound award for her capture or not.

The generally illiterate men had on the whole a very fine idea of the amount of prize money they might expect to be getting – eventually.

William swallowed some breakfast standing on the quarterdeck; a position of no dignity but the better to stay alert. He scarcely noticed what he was eating; command of a prize was one thing but care of a young lady was the most frightening duty he had ever had wished on him! A beautiful young lady who....

A beautiful young lady who played havoc with the set of his uniform; well that he could understand in this Burkett fellow, but to be captain of a ship he had to have more years and maturity than a very junior lieutenant and should surely have more self control! William was determined that Miss Finch would have no cause for complaint under HIS command.

His equilibrium was to be further undermined when Miss Finch tripped up the ladder to the quarterdeck twirling an outrageously fringed apricot parasol and wearing ridiculous lace-covered apricot satin gloves, her silky curls covered by a bonnet of white ruched silk and trimmed with apricot ribbons to match those on her gown..

He bowed.

"Miss Finch" he said "You appear all set for a promenade in the park; I fear I cannot oblige you in that respect. However if imagination would turn the mizzen mast into a fine beech tree and lay grass upon the deck you may enjoy your promenade."

Miss Finch gave a gurgle of mirth that made all the giggles William had ever heard sound commonplace and vulgar.

"You are quite absurd, Mr Price!" she said "But then I am not averse to a little whimsy; observe if you will, in your imagination, a grassy sward filled with daisies and other gay flowers!"

"A delightful vista" said William gravely. "Alas that I am no botanist to put names to the flowers! Buttercups and daisies and dandelions and such weeds are I fear all I might recognise; childhood's favourites since before I went to sea!"

"And how old were you when you went to sea, Mr Price?" said Miss Finch.

"Oh a child of twelve – a little younger than Mr Prescott there, who is learning from Scully how to use the wheel" said William "Ah, and while we are about it; Mr Prescott, if the lady suffers from any practical jokes you had better beware my imagination"

"Aye aye sir" said Prescott regretfully.

A pity; ladies were usually such very good subjects to play jokes upon, they rose so well. And it wasn't like disrupting the crew.

"Is Mr Price sweet on the Yankee lady?" he asked Scully in an undertone.

"Mr Prescott, might I trouble you to keep a civil tongue about your captain in your horrid little mouth, sir" said Scully "Or I might have to recommend to him that you need more coaching in mathematics."

"Damn your eyes Scully!" said Prescott in what he hoped was the manner of Captain Mornington.

"Aye sir" said Scully, impassively.

William was wondering what to say to Miss Finch, or indeed if it were proper to say anything to Miss Finch when the lookout hailed.

"Deck there! Sail on the horizon astern; closing on us!"

"Mr Prescott" said William "perhaps I may trouble you to take the bring-em-near aloft."

The boy sprang for the ratlines with the telescope; and shortly called down,

"Deck! She has American colours; 'tis a three-masted schooner! 'Thrush' has signalled the same!"

"Acknowledge and come down!" William called "Well at least the men have had breakfast" he added philosophically. "Tom, pass the word to beat to quarters; Miss Finch I must trouble you to go below. Your countrymen are about to try to rescue you and this ship. And I should really lock you in your cabin" he added.

"I don't know enough to cause you to lose a sea battle without killing myself" said Miss Finch, coldly. "Do you have to beat the men to get them to go to quarters, whatever that is? I thought you were a kindly man"

William stared.

"It is a drum that is beaten" he said "You may hear it now. Quarters is to summon the men to man the guns. Scully, you'll have to go aloft; I'll take the wheel myself. I can't lose a decent topsman."

"Sir" said Scully "You'll not man all the guns either."

"No; but we've practised firing one, then another, leaving one man to swab out" said William. "Miss Finch go below; you are in danger on deck; I mean it."

Miss Finch took a look at his serious face, curtseyed, and withdrew. And the schooner was catching up.

Chapter 14

"Mr Prescott," said William hoping he sounded calm, "see that all the guns are loaded. The crews must serve one broadside at a time, but since we are only fighting one ship that should suffice. You are in charge of the gun crews. I'll keep an eye out for the signals from 'Thrush' myself."

"Aye aye sir!" said Prescott darting off. At least with all the guns on the upper deck, William thought, he could oversee the action from where he was. 'Thrush' was signalling; it was a word spelled out. William squinted at the flags against the now bright sky.

13-21-19-3-17-1-3-10-5-17

Nutcracker.

Nutcracker? Unorthodox signal but quite clear – if one knew Captain Mornington.

"Scully's compliments sir," squeaked the ship's boy, "and would I remind you that he passed the word about the 'Thrush' being down at the head and organised the movement of cargo forward to trim us, too, sir."

"My compliments to Scully and tell him he's possibly saved our bacon" said William with heartfelt gratitude.

He had been mesmerised by the fair captive and Scully had managed to tell Captain Mornington what it had been *his* place to do.... And doubtless told the Captain that 'Mr Price wished you to know, sir....' Into the bargain.

There was so much to remember when one was in charge; *too* much to remember. No, it was not too much; other captains managed it. He was just hopelessly inept as yet. Scully would have done a better job...

No, Scully had not the experience of seamanship; but he would make a fine captain one day if prejudice did not prevent it. Scully had near total recall; doubtless he had read the flags already and relayed the message to the others aloft. Now what was coming up?

648-605-820 'prize pass astern'.

That sort of nutcracker. Scully did not have the signal book but the number 648 had been used to call them before, and he was bound to know astern.... There was a ragged cheer up in the shrouds; and William raised a hand to acknowledge that he appreciated their enthusiasm. Scully would be watching him on the wheel..... if he turned to port and used the wind and if the 'Thrush' came up a couple of points on the port side he might come round behind the larger schooner. It was risky and called for being pretty close hauled and if they got into stays they would be dead. They did not have to *take* the schooner; only persuade a privateer that it was not worth his while and the cost of repairs to persevere.

The men would be disappointed of course but if they seriously expected a sloop and a schooner-sloop to take a three-master, probably almost as much in displacement tons as both the other ships they might be being unduly optimistic.

"Sir?" Tom had run up "Sir, Peters says it's more'n an 'undred feet he thinks, and he reckons a broadside of eight guns, he reckons nine-pounders, sir, but Scully says they look like six pounders to him."

"Thank you Tom" said William.

If they were nine pounders they may as well kiss goodbye to the world; but even larger schooners rarely carried anything larger than six-pounders. The 'Thrush' carried twelve nine-pounders and a twelve-pounder bowchaser, as well as the four twelve-pounder carronades, two each on the quarterdeck and at the fo'c'sle that did not count when reckoning the number of guns because they were not long guns and were only of use at close range. Sloops were built to survive something of a pounding; and Captain Mornington, by putting himself across the bows of the enemy would be in range for a broadside from them first before the more vulnerable 'Mosquito' schooner. Moreover the dozen or so swivel guns the 'Thrush' carried aimed at the enemy's sails might manage to damage the sails sufficiently to hinder the bigger ship's manoeuvrability.

Well he had the use of twelve six-pounders and a nine-pounder bow chaser, which was of itself unlikely to be of much use.

Unless......

"Lads!" he called "Get that nine-pounder to the middle of the starboard side!"

They would be firing on the starboard broadside first; it was worth making that count. William watched young Prescott set to organising moving guns about; one had to admit that given a practical task the boy was quite equal to it.

They were about to pass the enemy schooner going the other way; the distance was considerable but there was still some risk. William was impressed by the way Captain Mornington had guessed that the privateer would want to try to cripple the better armed Royal Navy ship first before trying to take back the 'Mosquito'; it had led to the bigger schooner taking exactly the right course that would enable the manoeuvre to work.

William reflected that he must be careful in writing his log that he interpreted the single word in light of conversations held over dinner in the great cabin and so an unorthodox order had made perfect sense. He had no idea whether they had indeed had such discussions but it would cover the Captain and then if anything went wrong his log might be able to testify in the Captain's defence if it came to a court martial.

He duly scrawled his thoughts in his day book, tying the wheel briefly to do so.

"Mr Price"

Miss Finch's voice came through the skylight.

"Miss Finch?" William tried not to sound impatient.

"Mr Price I am very nervous here below; I should be very much happier if I could see the danger clearly; if I promise my parole and to stay out of your way, may I come back on deck?"

William thought quickly.   It must be absolutely terrifying alone and below.

"Very well, Miss Finch providing you will also promise to do exactly what I order should there be occasion to do so. And also that you carry your ridiculous parasol to make it clear that you are a lady to anyone shooting at us."

"I will Mr Price" said Miss Finch sounding relieved.

She tripped lightly back on deck with her parasol and a cushion to sit on and took herself aft.

"Good girl" said William, smiling approval.

She pouted slightly.

"Was that intended to be patronising sir?" she asked.

"No Miss Finch; I'd say the same to my favourite sister." said William, "and right now that's how I'm planning on treating you. Now no more conversation if you please: I have a ship to fight."

"Aye aye sir" said Miss Finch with some irony.

The men on the after carronades were grinning; William decided to ignore them.

There was the little matter of the big schooner after all; and the possibility of a broadside from it.

The puffs of smoke from its side told that the enemy had decided to engage what seemed long seconds before the thunder of the guns and whistle of a cannon ball – the only one that reached – came overhead to pierce a hole in one of the sails. There was a scream and one of the men aloft, taken unawares by the jerk to the sail, lost his balance and fell.

There was a collective gasp from the men.

"Mr Price, I could tend him" said Miss Finch.

"He won't live but you have permission to comfort him if he is alive" said William.

She darted forwards.

The men in the tops and the men on the cannon were plainly afraid; after all, most of them had never seen battle. William cursed under his breath; how could he stiffen them?

Scully's voice bellowed from the tops.

"Hold fast boys! We have to fight to save Miss Finch from these rapacious pirates!"

He evidently added something to the crew aloft too for there was a guffaw.

William strongly suspected it was some reference to saving the virginity of their Prize Captain too; well, if it kept the men in good heart, what they said about him was not important, so long as they respected him enough to follow his orders.

"Thank you Scully!" called William "The Royal Navy always protects ladies!"

It was not to be expected that six pounders could do much at two miles; even if fired with the accuracy the Royal Navy expected of her gunners. The privateers were used to closing on clumsy merchantmen and intimidating them.

They had nearly succeeded with his men too.

Prescott ran aft, and saluted.

"Permission to return the broadside, sir?" he said.

"Denied" said William "We are not in effective range – one nine-pounder is not sufficient on the side of the ship. We carry out orders and rake her stern with all fire. We'll be firing back; now get back to your men!"

Prescott saluted and ran off, almost tripping over the ridiculous dirk when it got between his legs.

He had a lot to learn.

Just because they were just about in range did NOT mean that it was a good time to fire; and doubtless the broadside at the 'Mosquito' had been intended to intimidate a reduced prize crew.

"Stand by to come about lads!" bellowed William "We have a pirate to defeat who thinks he can intimidate good British lads!"

"Some of whom are French!" he heard Haybean call.

"A blow for the Old World, Haybean!" William returned.

There was laughter; that was better. Sailors in a jocular mood would forget their fear.

Miss Finch came aft.

"That's one lucky man" she said "He bounced off the sail a couple of times on the way down; I don't think he's done worse than break his leg. I tied both legs together to keep it straight and gave him water."

"Good girl" approved William.

The man might have internal injuries too; there again he might be the luckiest man in the world. Odd things sometimes happened at sea.

The next few minutes were going to be vital.

They were coming up into the wind and would be close hauled as they crossed it, and if luck – and seamanship – were against them they would end up in stays, wallowing like a grounded whale while the 'Thrush' took the brunt of the attack, and then possibly still helpless when the Schooner – her name he thought he could by squinting make out to be Nancy-Beth – came to pluck them like a ripe piece of fruit. All of Starboard watch were rated Ordinary Seaman however, even Wick, who had struggled through his tests. Scully was largely responsible for this. William hoped that Scully's first battle would not be his last; the man had a lot to give the navy.

He pulled the wheel round at the moment he judged the best – and that was one of the things Scully must learn to be an officer, judging the best timing – and the sailors aloft trimmed the sails in a frenzy of activity, so small as they looked so far up and so vital in their activities for the plan to work.

They were coming across the wind; a brief flog; and through it; and the gaffs had caught the wind, and now the courses. They were running lightly, skittishly; making almost as much sideways movement as headway but that was also in the plan. They would pass astern the 'Nancy-Beth' – a wife, or a sweetheart or a daughter? Wondered

William – initially just shy of a quarter mile. A little more distant than he might like; but the gunners were good and the stern of any ship was vulnerable even to light six pounders. And the angle they were taking they would be racing closer as the passed.

"Starboard battery; fire as your guns bear!" called William.

The big schooner was shuddering; holes appeared in her sails.

The 'Thrush' had turned and blasted the 'Nancy-Beth' with her broadside and the swivels were shredding her courses to make manoeuvring harder.

It would also kill enemy sailors.

The detonation of 'Mosquito's' own first gun, almost made William jump.

The deck shook under the vibration; or maybe that was his imagination. William had been in battle before but this was the first time in command, and somehow he felt curiously detached for not having a specific task as Mr Prescott had HIS specific task of encouraging the gun crews and filling in if necessary.

And then the next; then the long nine pounder, crewed by the best and steadiest gun crew, her heavy shot crashing into the weaker stern of the ship. Then one by one the other three six pounders and the carronade on the quarterdeck, now in range as they came closer, barely a cable's length away, bringing the broadside to a deafening crescendo!

The crew of the first gun had already swabbed out and reloaded and were turning the gun to get a second shot before they were passed; the second gun crew were not going to make it.

The nine-pounder – by George, they were almost as fast as the first team! A second nine-pound ball into the schooner captain's cabin was going to spoil his day!

"Why the ends?" asked Miss Finch.

"Less protected" said William "This ship is more than a match for our two ships unless we could come up with something like this. Also the shot can career the whole length of the ship doing a considerable amount of damage inside. It's not pretty, ma'am; you have to recall these pirates might just consider you property as much as that bast – er, fellow – Burkett and that wouldn't be pretty either. If you can't stand to see it go below."

"I can stand it" said Miss Finch. "I've had my protected eyes opened rather a lot. I want to cheer for my fellow Americans but I can't help thinking that you might be right about how they would treat me. I don't like you or them very much right now."

"No ma'am" said William. There was not a lot else to say; and he could scarcely blame her for antipathy towards both sides.

The Schooner had stern chasers as well as bow chasers; and as he expected they were now firing.

The bulwark by number one gun vanished in smithereens and men screamed.

"I'll go help" said Miss Finch.

William did not stop her. The surgeon – Campbell's best loblolly boy, the horse doctor – was also on his way, but a young lady nurse would not hurt. She would comfort the dying if nothing else just by her presence, especially if, as Scully intimated, they had taken her to heart to protect.

One could never fathom how sentimental rough sailors could sometimes be.

William looked to his steering; the wind was in the right quarter, they could come about again, put the wind behind them and rake the stern from the larboard broadside.

"Stand by to go about!" he cried. "Gun crews to the Larboard battery!"

The men – the survivors – ran across the deck to the other side of the ship to wait, ready by the guns. Sensibly, Mr Prescott ordered the crews to the guns that would bear first, the crew to run down to fire the one that would bear last.

The ship heeled as he swung the wheel; the men aloft performed their arcane aerial ballet; and the 'Mosquito's' guns were thundering again, the stern chasers of the 'Nancy-Beth' ready this time.

William noticed in slow motion as they passed under her transom the name picked out in gold, and missing the first two letters of the name where one of their holes was. They were a lot closer this time.

The world exploded around him and things went black.

Chapter 15

William came to with Miss Finch bathing his face. She looked like an angel.

"Only heaven wouldn't have such beautiful angels" said William groggily.

"Lie still Mr Price; you were hit on the head by a lump of flying wood and knocked out" said Miss Finch.

William sat up and regretted it.

He vomited, managing to turn away to miss vomiting on the angel.

"I TOLD you to lie still!" said Miss Finch with some asperity.

"Lying still, Miss Finch" said William in a voice that sounded ridiculously weak to his own ears "Is a luxury not afforded the commander of a vessel. Your father would not do so."

She regarded him thoughtfully.

"No he would not" she said "Then permit me to help you."

William decided it was no time for pride and let her take his arm and assist him to his shaky feet.

The scene was not one of the carnage he had feared; indeed it hardly seemed much changed from before he had been knocked witless. There was a missing chunk of bulwark on the quarterdeck; one of the carronade crew had taken the wheel; and the 'Mosquito' was moving steadily past the stern of the 'Nancy-Beth' out of the arc of her stern chasers which appeared in any case to be quiescent.

Mr Prescott came aft and saluted.

"Sir, the forward carronade crew wish to report that they claim the enemy's stern chaser" he said breathlessly.

"Tell them I'm extremely grateful" said William "They can have an extra tot tonight."

Prescott grinned.

He had learned enough to know that they would value the Prize Captain's gratitude above the tot.

The Privateer was turning. It was turning on a course that would intercept the 'Mosquito'.

"*HELLFIRE*" said William, forgetting that Miss Finch was there.

If they continued on this course and speed, 'Nancy-Beth' would be in a position to rake them from stem to stern for taking her broadside across their bows.

"Are we going to die?" asked Miss Finch.

The girl had not a tremor to her voice! It steadied William.

"Not if I can help it" he said "ALL HANDS! GET ALL SAIL REPEAT, ALL SAIL!"

His shouting felt as though each word were being fired at the inside of his skull with roundshot attached and he groaned and held his head.

Miss Finch passed him a wetted rag which he held gratefully to the most insistent part of the headache where the greater number of unsecured round shot appeared to be rolling back and forth in his skull as they would on deck if left unsecured.

"What is your plan?" she asked.

He should not really tell her; but if it had a flaw it would be better to say it out loud to someone….

"If we let 'Nancy-Beth' cross our 'T' – sail across our bow – she can use her broadside to effectively gut this ship; so I want to get ahead of her and not be cut off from our fellow, the 'Thrush' any more. We will pass extremely close down 'Nancy-Beth's' side but I am hoping that their guns will not depress far enough to be able to fire at us. The *risky* bit is as we pass her bow."

"Why, I'm glad that being within handshake of all those guns isn't the risky bit!" said Miss Finch. Her voice shook slightly but she was endeavouring to sound gay.

William gave her an approving smile.

"You are a brave lady" he said "No, the risky bit is as we cut across her bows and hope that we can get enough speed on us that even when we come into her lee – the wind can't reach us because her bulk blocks it – we will keep going long enough to pick up the wind again as we clear the bow and that she doesn't run us down."

"That is risky" said Miss Finch "But it's the same with trade; who plays safe never gains, papa always says. Will it help when we are in the lee if I go and fetch my fan to ply vigorously?" her dark eyes twinkled.

"Well it might help the lads to feel better about it" said William "They appreciate a sense of humour; and you never know, as sailors are often superstitious, they might believe you could charm a few bits of wind for us."

"Then I shall fetch a fan" said Miss Finch "For I think that may be better help for morale than helping the wounded. By the way, what did they laugh about after Mr Scully told them to protect me?"

"He is currently not rated 'Mr'" said William "Though I believe he has ability to be an officer and I'm working on helping him get there. I suspect he passed a coarse jest at my expense for the crew. He's a gentleman; he'd not jest at a lady's expense, if that was what you wondered."

"I did" admitted Miss Finch "How come a gentleman is a common sailor?"

"Long story; and his to tell not mine" said William "He told me in confidence."

"Then of course you must not break that confidence" nodded Miss Finch and tripped away for her fan.

The sails had filled and made 'Mosquito' jump forward like, as William's knowledge of Shakespeare made him think, 'the greyhounds at their slips' or rather having been released from the slips, or collars. The Dominie at his grammar school had read exciting things to them if as a class they got a consistently high mark in Latin; it had been an incentive to work hard and help the dullards. Really he should not think of such inconsequential things when he must concentrate to the full to fight the ship! They were converging on the 'Nancy-Beth', they would almost scrape her bulwarks with the lower spars by the time the were at the other end of her. Faster and faster..... it was her sails that would make most of the lee, she was only a deck taller than the 'Mosquito'.

"Ready fan.... DEPLOY FAN MISS FINCH" he gave the order, entering into her humour for the sake of the men. She made a pretty picture fluttering a ridiculous confection of lace; but if it was the last picture the men had, it would be one that had them laughing in delight at least. And then he realised there was something he had not taken into account.

"GET DOWN FROM ALOFT!" he bellowed.

The men were obeying, running down the rigging; and William was shouting at the men on the quarterdeck, picking up Miss Finch and jumping clear down the steps to the deck and thrusting her up into the entrance to the great cabin.

The mainmast cleared the bowsprit of the bigger schooner; but the mizzen mast did not.

With a splintering crash it fell onto the quarterdeck, the sails dragging in the sea abaft the 'Mosquito'.

William grabbed a boarding axe to cut away rigging, and saw others helping, Wick severing ropes with single, powerful strokes, to separate them from the American ship.

He heard a roar of cannon and wondered why he was still chopping when they had surely been reduced to matchwood by the 'Nancy-Beth'.

And his own men were cheering...

Suddenly he realised that Mr Prescott had taken it upon his insolent, thirteen-year-old shoulders to order the Larboard battery to fire, sails and cordage all over the place despite.

And the American ship was listing severely.

An officer ran to the bows.

"Limey scum! We will not surrender!" he cried "Board us at your peril; we can still fight!"

"I have no intention of boarding you, you Yankee scum!" said William "I don't know what I might catch! Sheer off; I don't want your damned ship; and you can tell the pirate Burkett if I ever meet him, I think his attitude to ladies is loathsome and uncivilised and I shall be glad to meet him any time, any place!"

"And you can tell him I spit on him!" said Miss Finch who was wielding an axe with more vigour than accuracy.

"And if I were you, I'd get your men to the pumps" said William "Now go away; you rebel colonials bore me."

"Not all of them sir" murmured one of those cutting rigging, with a glance at Miss Finch.

"Damn your eyes, Dempsey" said William dredging up the man's name.

"You know me name sir? Oh sir!" Dempsey beamed all over his face; and William was glad he had gone to the trouble of learning all the names.

The mess of cordage being cut free, William ordered men aloft to the foremast to stabilise the sails; and partially furl them. Carrying the whole weight of the ship would put a strain on the smaller foremast and could cause it to break with too great a press of canvas.   The American ship was sufficiently crippled at least that all they wanted to do was limp away; and as 'Thrush' came up to stand protectively by 'Mosquito' it was tacitly agreed that the large schooner should be permitted to leave.   'Thrush' could reduce her to matchwood and drown every last man aboard not killed by shot or flying splinters, but at the price of the schooner destroying the equally crippled 'Mosquito' in revenge.

Privateers would accept the trade off. And Mornington would not abandon those of his men on the smaller ship just to count a privateer sunk. It would be a long time before the 'Nancy-Beth' would be fully seaworthy again.

The Lords of the Admiralty would doubtless have preferred two American ships sunk   including the Mosquito; but this was not their decision and Mornington would answer for it later, signalling to 648, the prize, to cease engagement.

That way it was an order and William would not be in trouble; and William appreciated that.

And if it came to court martial he would declare that their own troubles looked worse than they were and the Captain wished to send assistance to his own men on the prize.

Boats were sent out from the 'Thrush' as the American ship limped away; how odd it was to have Captain Mornington ask permission to come aboard!

That was rapidly given and Mornington glanced around.

"Miscalculation or calculated risk?" he asked.

"Sir, the calculated risk was passing under her bow without being rammed, I plain forgot the mast and her bowsprit" said William.

"An honest answer. You took a calculated risk to save your ship and crew; it cost a mast rather than costing the ship" said Mornington.   "A fair trade.   Making any decision is better than making no decision. The carpenter and his mate are coming over to help you jury-rig a mast. Ever done it before?"

"No sir, but I've seen it done, when I was serving on a ship that lost a mast in the back end of a hurricane, in the Caribbean" said William.

"Then you won't want my interference" said Mornington. "Don't hesitate however to ask if you're unsure of yourself; you're still learning. Rapidly if I may say so. You'll have a romantic scar, my boy; good job you're as blonde as a guinea or the ladies might take you for some hero of a gothic novel! The brooding romantic heroes are however all *darkly* brooding."

William laughed.

"I don't have any fancy to be Byronesque or taken for some lord of a tumbledown castle with a deep family secret" he said. "Will there be trouble over letting the Jonathon go?"

"Hector is pessimistic but I fancy their lordships will be so pleased to have a nippy little craft like the 'Mosquito' we might not be censured too heavily" said Mornington. "Will I get a slap on the wrist for not pounding her? Yes. But not risking the destruction of a craft that is more than a schooner but a good cock of the snoot at America will weigh for more. It's not as though we took her in battle – even though that would be harder – but that she was cut out under their noses. What's your butcher's bill?"

"I'm waiting for it to be brought up" said William, glad he had sent little Tom running to ask for it. "My horse doctor can only count if he's allowed to do it by stamping his hooves."

Mornington laughed.

"Poor man; he's quite adequate at splinting fetlocks however" he said.

"And I *am* quite literate, Captain" said Miss Finch coming up to the officers "I went with Tom to find out the dead and wounded. Four men died from the first shot that hit us; the man that fell has no more than a broken leg; and one man from that first blow is to lose an arm; er, Horse I believe he is called, would like him transferred to a Mr Campbell's care. The blow that knocked Mr Price out has caused splinter damage to two men, and caused a crushed foot from a dismounted carronade. Horse says we had light casualties."

"Yes Ma'am; that's quite right" said Mornington. "The 'Thrush' also was lucky, losing only half a dozen men to the first onslaught. We set out of course to take the brunt, being the sturdier ship; and not having a lady on board."

"Well I have seen the devastation the 'Mosquito' can cause on an unarmed merchantman" said Miss Finch. "I will ask you gentlemen to excuse me; I believe I wish to lie down."

"You will do well to drink a glass of water first and then another after you have finished crying" said William "So I was advised after the first battle I saw. Perhaps you'd take Tom to run errands for you too; I'm sure he could do with light duties."

She managed a tremulous smile.

"You are a kind man" she said "What of Mr Prescott?"

"I'll give him the same advice and let him shed any tears in manly solitude" said William "He is an officer and a gentleman."

She nodded.

"Well…. thank you" she said; and retired, calling for little Tom.

"Handy supernumery by the looks of it" said Mornington.

"She gave the men the morale they needed" said William seriously. "Wish I could sign her on sir!"

"Well well! Make sure you write up your reports in good time" said Mornington nodding to him as he prepared to depart.

A wise captain did not interfere too much in a young prize captain's command.

And William appreciated being permitted to keep the command that could have been passed to Hector Phrayle.

Chapter 16

Miss Finch was dismissed forward after she next emerged while the jury-mast was fitted. The old mast had been cut away below – she had heard the saws – to permit the jury rig to be fitted, or 'stepped' as she heard them say. Apparently as the old mast had not gone by the board – fallen over the edge – they were able to trim it down and use it again, losing some of its height. This seemed to Miss Finch an eminently sensible way to go about things and not in the least profligate. She sat by the mainmast with her embroidery and neglected it to watch the industry of the big A-frames being constructed; and a good name it was as they looked like the capital letter 'A'. Various arcane cats-cradles of ropes were set up through the pulleys that she knew were called blocks.

Mr Prescott told her importantly that every block reduced by half the weight that had to be lifted and so with three blocks rigged together that meant a sixth of the weight and now he could see it done it made more sense and he shouldn't ever find himself caned for not knowing again.

When everything was in place, the sailors attached the main rope to the capstan and walked around it pushing on the capstan bars to winch the mast slowly but surely upright,, while one man stood on the capstan and played a fiddle to get them pulling in rhythm. And up came the mast, dropped into the hole – was stepped rather – and then all kinds of ropes were attached to the great dead-eyes – an evocatively macabre name – on the bulwarks.

And then it was the funerals of the men who had died.

Miss Finch had never attended a funeral at sea; she was surprised at how moving it was, having rather assumed that the Royal Navy treated its men as expendable, and not caring about their individual needs. She had half expected a single brief tribute and the five bodies put overboard together but to her surprise this was not the case.

The men had been sewn into their own hammocks with several roundshot to make sure they sank; and little Tom told her with all the pleasurable ghoulishness of a ten year old small boy that the sailmaker passed the last stitch through the nose to make sure that corpse was really dead since that would wake up any unconscious person or at least make them bleed.

There was a grisly sort of good sense in that, especially on ships where there was no proper surgeon or physician.

The ensign was lowered to half mast as the drum summoned the hands. Each body was placed on a plank on the standing part of the foresheet with the union flag over the canvas bundle that had once been a man; and the Captain – Mr Price – asked a messmate for a brief word about the dead man. He then said a brief prayer and the plank was tilted to permit the body to slide into the sea.

William called for the singing of 'Hearts of Oak' to round off the funeral mindful of the irony of the lines 'Tis to honour we call you, not press you like slaves, for who are as free as the sons of the waves' since half at least of the men, if not pressed, had at least found little option in joining up; however the seamen sang it heartily enough and did not appear to resent the ironies at all.

Then when he had dismissed the men he beckoned Scully over.

"Scully, you've been acting cox; and you're the only man on board who can add up a column of figures without a muddle, not excluding me. It's the cox'n's job to auction off the possessions of a dead man to add some money to his estate. Don't be surprised that the possessions usually fetch much more than their value, or that often they are returned to be sold a second time. This is the way the men can materially help out widows and orphans."

"Aye aye sir" said Scully softly. "There's a lot more in being a sailor than you'd think, isn't there?"

"There is Scully" said William "And the thing that should always be remembered, whatever the Lords of the Admiralty might believe, is that a sailor is also a man."

"Aye sir" said Scully. "Is it true that the success of an operation is marked by them by the size of the butcher's bill?"

William sighed.

"So it is said, Scully, and I've seen enough promotions or plum appointments go to men who spent their men's lives like water to dispute it. The theory goes, I suppose, that if many men died to achieve an objective, it was paid for and therefore worth the cost. They don't take into account men like Captain Mornington who try to reduce the butcher's bill by cleverness. And Cochrane" he added.

"And you sir" said Scully. "And I see that the risky and bold action can actually save more lives than the vacillating one."

"Yes" said William "I wish to model myself after those who do their best not to spend lives – but not by being an old woman, skulking and afraid to take action. Because you are correct. A bold action *can* often succeed and do so, because of surprise, with minimal loss of life. But far too many officers dare not risk court martial by taking a bold decision. You cannot be court martialled for following the last set of orders or sticking strictly to regulations. And when you are a midshipman you will have to decide if you are going to take risks or sit out your career safely."

"I don't think, sir, that there is any choice" said Scully "He who never ventured, never gained. My venture in forgery was a failure; I paid for that. I had an impeccable witness against me because I wasn't bold enough. Had I been bolder and actually added the codicil in working hours in front of everyone's eyes I should probably have got away with it. Working late aroused suspicions."

"Well I have to say I agree" said William "But the navy would have lost a fine potential officer. I do however deeply regret that your mother lost her life through it."

"I suppose I cannot guarantee that a doctor would have helped her" said Scully "But it is something I will always resent. I sometimes cheer myself up with the idea of being on a press-gang that presses that sanctimonious clerk."

William grinned.

"I can see the attraction!" he said. "Well, away and sort out those belongings; we've a nice stiff breeze, the jury mast is holding firm and we shan't need any sail handling for a while."

"Aye aye sir" said Scully.

The run back to England was uneventful, as well it might be with the war against France over. William spoke to Captain Mornington about letting Miss Finch's father know she was safe; and Captain Mornington altered course to intercept a Dutch merchantman to see about having Miss Finch's letter delivered safely.

It may be said that the Prize Crew considered themselves privileged to have such a lovely young lady on board, especially since Miss Finch had helped with the wounded. And the seaman who had fallen from aloft considered her a positive talisman and swore that her rapid ministrations to him saved his leg as well as her presence saving his life.

As to the latter this was pure superstition; but as to the former, William would not have been ready to dispute his guess! A well set broken leg, done quickly, could mean the leg healing straight with only the odd twinge in bad weather. One left unset could tear muscle and fester and might indeed mean losing the leg.

Though as Scully said privately to William, the vision most of the men had was of Miss Finch, parasol in one hand as though to fend off boarders and boarding axe ineffectively wielded in the other.

"Charmingly ineffective womanhood but doing what she might" he said cynically.

"Frankly Scully, I'd rather have Miss Finch as a recruit than a significant number of the young gentlemen I've known" said William.

Scully laughed.

He was unable to be rated Able Seaman since he had less than two years sea time; but Captain Mornington had promised to do all he could to arrange for him to have a warrant as Midshipman as soon as could be, hopefully in time for the next cruise. Technically one needed three years sea time to be a midshipman and must start as a volunteer, first class; but considering the way the system was abused with boys as young as five years old carried on the books only and not at sea at all to give them supposed sea time, Mornington was sure he could find a way around that. But he must serve his six years before he might seek promotion. Mornington was of the opinion that it took that long to learn enough and experience enough to be worthy to be a lieutenant, whether one had enough theoretical knowledge to pass the examination or not.

It meant that Scully would be thirty before he might stand for the lieutenant's exams but at least he would be in a situation where his initiative could be put to good use without the necessary constraints of being one of the men.

"Will you come with me as my cox and servant on shore if we have any leave?" William asked him. "I want to take Miss Finch somewhere safe, and I have made up my mind that the best place for her is with my sister, who will doubtless be married by now, to our cousin Edmund. He's a vicar; and a good man."

"Sounds like they are just the people to care for her sir" said Scully "I'd be honoured to travel with you."

"And if the warrant comes through I'll go with you to outfit you" said William. "Make sure the outfitters don't try to fob you off with unnecessary kit or leave anything out. You know."

Scully laughed dryly.

"Oh I know" he said. "Thank you sir. I hope that I might sail with you as a trainee officer."

The crew of the 'Thrush' and the prize crew of the 'Mosquito' found themselves temporary heroes once they had returned to Portsmouth to dock; for the iniquities and impudence of the American privateers, operating even off the coast of Wales, was a cause célèbre; and the equal audacity of Royal Navy sailors made them the darlings of the public imagination. Which, as Captain Mornington said with a droll smile, might offset any censure for irregularities.

William had spent much time writing up his reports and making sure the log was up to date and all the paperwork was duly returned to be perused with a careful eye to irregularity and no eye at all to intellect, as he told Scully.

"The navy board sails paper boats upon a sea of ink" he said dryly.

"At least they don't go to sea sir" said Scully "Think of the mess they'd make of it!"

"Oh very nice, Scully, very nice!" laughed William. "Well, we shall have word soon if we might go ashore; it's seventy miles from London to Mansfield, and almost as far from Portsmouth to London; and if we post we may do it in just a few days. I will not subject Miss Finch to the rigours of the Mailcoach, even though it would be faster, not unless our time here is to be curtailed. Which it cannot be likely to be for we require repairs to the 'Thrush' as well."

They had returned to the 'Thrush' while the 'Mosquito' was to be haggled over and the prize money to be decided upon. Captain Mornington had given up his cabin to Miss Finch – she had refused to go on shore with strangers – and took Hector Phrayle's cabin, Hector bunking in with William cheerfully.

"It was wonderful experience, Hector" said William "Thank you for letting me try command."

"You're welcome laddie" said Phrayle "Mind, if I'd known you were going to pick up the prettiest girl without a fish's tail to be found in the ocean I might have argued more!"

William laughed.

"Do you think me presumptuous to take her to my sister?" he said .

"Not at all lad; the Captain's a widower – doesn't speak about it, but his wife died in childbed – and I've no suitable female relatives. She should technically be returned to America of course but I can quite see that if she was packed off to Europe for her own safety in the first place, she'd be loath to go. But you won't mind if I see if I might fix an interest with her?"

"Oh, it's not my place to mind" said William "She shall make up her own mind whether she should flirt with either one of us or not at all; she's too young to even think of serious beaux I think" he added.

"That'll change by next time we're in England I wager!" laughed Phrayle.

Chapter 17

"Miss Finch, I hesitate to ask this, because it's a little personal" said William blushing.

"Dear me" said Miss Finch "*How* personal?"

"It is concerning how you are financially placed without the funds of your father at your disposal" said William bluntly "Since you should really engage a maid to travel with you and I am not a wealthy man."

"Oh is that all!" said Miss Finch "I am what is generally known as tolerably well blunted; papa knew I should want to buy geegaws in Paris so he gave me a goodly amount of money; and for all his piracy, Burkett had both my trunks brought aboard. I split it up amongst my possessions to hide it and in reticules so that if anything occurred – I was thinking about a carriage accident in France, I have to say, not piracy – I might have a number of reticules each containing some. Papa sent me with a year's allowance, so I have ten thousand dollars on me in French banknotes."

"Good G-d" said William blankly. "I had no idea! If I had known that you had that much I should have surely been too terrified to guard you on the trip! It is a fortune! We must have it exchanged to pounds for you in London; that will prove no difficulty. That is enough to live well with servants for four years at least even without somewhere ready to stay; I hope you will not, in that case, mind helping with the household expenses in my sister and brother-in-law's house for they would be stretched to take in another young lady otherwise. Of course they would do so if you were as temporarily destitute as I supposed you" he added hastily.

She smiled.

"If they are as good as you say, Mr Price, I think your relatives sound wonderful people" she said, "And I will be glad to contribute. Will there be a school I might attend to do a year's finishing do you think?"

"Oh I am sure we can leave that in Edmund's capable hands" said William. "I can send Scully to advertise for a young person as your maid with a clear conscience then."

"Thank you" said Miss Finch.

Amelia Finch interviewed four applicants to be her maid, dismissed out of hand the two who looked scornfully on her dark skin, considered the politely spoken one that she feared might prove sly, and took on the young girl who exclaimed,

"Oh ma'am how beautiful you are, and how *exotic* you look!"

Kitty was utterly unsophisticated but Miss Finch had every expectation of training her up well; and besides an unsophisticated ingénue was preferable by far to a girl with possible sly tendencies.

They accordingly found themselves on the road with William and Scully; and Miss Finch had insisted on paying for the travel and accommodation on the way.

As he would normally travel on the mail, William had not demurred much.

The postchaise and its groom would change at every stop of course but that was not a problem; they would stay at posting inns where there were always other chaises for hire.

Miss Finch was awed by London; the size of it, the bustle, and the age of many of the buildings. William had never considered it before; but the oldest buildings in her own country were but seventeenth century and he found himself trying to recall what he knew of Westminster Abbey and found it easier to purchase a guide book.

"It says here that the site has been occupied since before the Norman conquest and the oldest part of the building was begun in 1245" breathed Miss Finch, having asked wistfully if they had time to spend an afternoon there after her banking needs had taken up the morning.

"Well, er, yes, I suppose so" said William "I never really thought about it; it's just Westminster Abbey you know."

"I suppose familiarity breeds contempt" sighed Miss Finch "*Do* try not to be so ignorant about it and take an interest!"

"I beg your pardon ma'am" said William gallantly "It is not that I am not interested in history; merely that I have never taken an interest in architecture."

"Well you wriggled like a worm on a hook to get out of that one amiably" said Miss Finch without rancour.

William laughed.

"I confess it" he said. "It is however fairly true; I've always been mad for the sea. If one of the ships of Henry VIII or better yet, those of Alfred the Great, might be available to go over then I should be boring you with the details a sailor needs years to learn; but you are right. I should take an interest in my country's heritage. It will make me appreciate the more what I am fighting for."

"Handsomely said, Mr Price" said Miss Finch.

William had sent a letter on ahead to Fanny and Edmund – having been to see his mother briefly to discover that they were indeed married – explaining the circumstances. Being used to writing reports in the most informative way and the least possible words, what his letter lacked in felicity of style was made up by the amount of information he managed to get onto one page without even crossing the letter.

And when they arrived at the big, homely rectory in Mansfield village, his dear sister Fanny ran out to embrace him, and then Miss Finch.

"Oh Miss Finch, do pray come inside; William is a dreadful correspondent but at least I have some idea of your straits!" she declared.

"Oh I wish you will call me Amelia, Mrs Bertram" said Miss Finch.

"And you must call me Fanny" said Fanny. "Oh how very lovely you are!"

"We make a handsome contrast" said Miss Finch noting that Fanny was as blonde as her brother "It is very kind of you to take me in; and I beg you to permit me to be a paying guest, for I was expecting to be so in France you know."

Fanny hesitated; it was not hospitable but the living of a country parson, even with a fine big rectory, was not such as permitted much over.

"I am sure we will come to some arrangement, Miss Finch, should you so wish, after you have spent some time purely as our guest" said Edmund, smiling.

Edmund was adroit at putting people at their ease; and William was grateful to him.

It was good to see his sister so happy.

"You are looking so well, Fanny" he said "Not that you looked at all anything but your lovely self last time I was home, but you looked sadly pulled, and not your sunny self. I'm glad you did not take that man Crawford even though his uncle is my patron."

"Oh William! I felt very guilty when he got you your promotion!" cried Fanny.

"You don't believe that lie do you?" said William in scorn "The *Navy* is not like the army you know; I had to pass an examination for my promotion and nobody got it for me but myself. And I had only just served long enough to apply for it in any case."

Fanny embraced him in delight.

"Then that is all I need to make my happiness complete!" she declared "Especially as I suspect," she blushed, "that you may be going to be an uncle!"

William grinned and nodded at his brother-in-law.

"Fast work, Edmund" he said.

Edmund blushed a little and laughed.

Amelia smiled.

They were a delightful and happy family; and she could help repay the hospitality too by helping when Fanny drew close to her confinement.

She was going to be very happy here; perhaps happier than in a school in France.

She must not feel guilty about the deaths of the men on the merchantman; but perhaps she could speak to the Reverend Bertram about that and about her feelings. He looked a good man; and he would perhaps pray with her for their souls, and for the souls of the men who had lost their lives in the battle with the 'Nancy-Beth'.

She sighed; Mr Price would be going back to sea soon, and she suddenly realised that even after so short a time, only a few weeks, she would miss him, and indeed Scully and Tom and Mr Prescott and all the sailors who had done their best to make her feel at home.

But he would have leaves.

And the war between their countries could not last forever; and then Mr Price and her father might meet. They were bound to be friends with so much in common!

And perhaps then Mr Price would have time to see her more often......

Miss Finch blushed prettily.

William Price and the Irish Problem

Chapter 1

"Oh this is too bad of William!" declared Mrs Fanny Bertram with some asperity as she brought in the morning mail.

"Why, my love, what has he done that you can tell even without opening the envelopes?" asked the Reverend Edmund Bertram mildly. He was surprised that his wife should express any kind of opprobrium towards her brother, whom she loved dearly.

Fanny sighed, and shook her head in fond exasperation.

"He has included a letter for Amelia; which not only have I had to pay for, as though sixpences grew on trees, but also which is most improper without obtaining permission from her father to correspond."

"I expect," said Amelia Finch, who was staying with the Bertrams, "that it was something to do with Mr Price saying that he would treat me like his favourite sister, because I reminded him of his sisters."

The comment had been made on the quarterdeck of the prize vessel 'Mosquito' the taking of which by Lieutenant Price had simultaneously made Miss Finch a captive of the British and rescued her from the piratical master of the 'Mosquito' who had kidnapped her. Miss Finch was resigned to spending any remaining time of the war against America in Britain rather than France where she had been headed, and thought herself fortunate to have such pleasant people as the Bertrams to be her host and hostess.

"That's all very well, but he should not be writing to a young lady who is *not* his sister" said Fanny. "Amelia, I am going to open this letter and read it; as your chaperone I have no choice. And I will write directly to William and direct him to write to the three of us as one since I will not permit him to compromise you in such a way! He forgets, having been on terms of easy intercourse with you at sea, that he must observe the proprieties; indeed being at sea without a respectable female with you is bad enough!"

"I guess that nobody could get up to much at sea without all the crew knowing" said Amelia "I had two dozen sailormen as my chaperones. My papa would understand me receiving mail under the circumstances, but it would be better if Mr Price might write under one letter."

She did not offer to pay for the letter; the Bertrams were proud. She would leave sixpence on Fanny's escritoire later and Fanny would give her a long hard look and she would smile brightly, and reluctantly Fanny would accept it. They had fallen into this easy way with each other very quickly; Miss Finch was a wealthy young woman and was happy to make sure that her presence did not financially embarrass her new friends.

Meanwhile Fanny had finished glancing over the letter and passed it on.

"It is quite unexceptionable," she said, "though my brother expects you to understand more nautical terms than those he inflicts on me."

Amelia laughed.

"Well my father *is* a shipowner" she said.

William received his sister's scolding letter with an addendum of a sentence or two from Miss Finch that she hoped he would be kind enough to add a word or two to her in any general letter that he sent; and sat down to scrawl off a rapid reply with an apology for behaving improperly, having never had occasion to correspond with a young lady before that he was not related to. It had to be a fast letter for they were due to sail with the next tide; but a vail to Yarde the coxswain had it taken ashore and set in the post.

There were two extra midshipmen on this voyage; one was John Scully, now in possession of the King's Warrant and if Captain Mornington had needed to talk fast, he had evidently managed it. William did not ask by what means the captain had overcome the small impediment of Scully not having three years sea time; it was doubtless by some casuistry or other, and had Scully been in prison for debts William might have imagined his captain blandly declaring him to have been at sea, without mentioning that the sea involved was the Marshalsea. However, somehow Mornington had overcome somebody's scruples to rank Scully Midshipman, not Volunteer First class.

There had been no court martial over the failure to capture or destroy the large American schooner; considering the moral advantage of bringing back a captured privateer as more advantageous than totally destroying a ship that might founder in any case had been considered good enough excuse. William had been mentioned in the Gazette for his bold actions and that was always a good step towards promotion!

The ship however was to be involved in fairly tedious and routine patrol work in the Irish Sea, to deter American privateers who had been treating it as their own pool so bold were they. Still, it would give Scully time to learn more and gain confidence in command.

William had seen to Scully's outfitting; and had helped out with the cost until such time as the prize money came through. The crew had done well out of the cruise, and it had completed the melding of them into a crew, because now they were behind a captain and officers who could bring them prize money! The captain had put up the sixty five pounds to purchase Scully's warrant too, which Scully was looking forward to paying back.

Captain Mornington had also taken what his superiors would have considered a massive risk of permitting shore leave by mess to all; and bar one man all had returned. Scuttlebutt was that other members of his own mess had tied up the unfortunate to prevent him from returning;

which was probably slander but showed that the deserter was held in general dislike. He had toadied to Wick when Wick was still a troublemaker and was inclined to tell tales to the bosun. Such seamen often got 'lost overboard'. He was the only man to regularly request a change of mess. Wick had certainly disliked him.

That was a man turned around; Wick was a man who had started off trying to make trouble for Scully and his followers as they learned from William's boy's seamanship manual that every midshipman owned; now as proud as punch of Scully for having made it to the Quarterdeck. And as grateful as any for the prize money!

It was not likely *this* cruise would be so profitable but that was the way it went.

William had not had much chance to assess the second new Midshipman; with a name like Arthur Ffarquar however the lad was probably related to someone who could lean on Admiral Crawford to have him assigned to a ship under one of the admiral's protégés. The youth had looked quite disgruntled and disgusted when he had been rowed over to the very small ship that was the Sloop of War 'Thrush'; Yarde, who had collected him, had shared this with the captain in the hearing of the two lieutenants, William and the first lieutenant, Hector Phrayle. The word was that the boy had been to the Naval Academy and his three years there had counted for two years sea time towards his seniority. William was not sure how he felt about that. Book learning was good, but to his mind, very little could really replace time at sea; for all the learning in the world could not instil in any boy or man the ability to smell a storm on the air, sense by the most minute sea changes that some weather change was afoot nor in battle judge at the last minute what an enemy captain had in mind.

By his manner, Mr Midshipman Ffarquar – which had already been rendered in William's unofficial hearing as Mr Midshipman Fartarse by the seamen – knew everything there was to know about the sea.

Well he would learn soon enough that he actually knew very little – unless the boy was accustomed to sailing on a relative's yacht.

Which would still not prepare him for the heaviest weather when yachts ran for shelter and warships just endured.

The Captain had all the officers, midshipmen included, to dine with him; the better, he said, to have their attention in the disclosure of their orders.

Mr Midshipman Ffarquar laughed dutifully.

Hector Phrayle, William and Scully nodded, as did the Sailing Master John Brigham, each acknowledging the mild witticism with a brief smile such as it warranted. Scully had observed that the Captain did not expect undue obsequiousness and that natural manners seemed appropriate, and Phrayle and William were used to Mornington's dry and understated manner. The younger midshipmen missed entirely that there had been a witticism and tried to look duly attentive. Mr Campbell the surgeon raised an eyebrow and left it at that.

Mornington threw a look of distaste at Ffarquar.

"Nothing exciting like sealed orders this time then sir?" ventured William. It was unlikely in the extreme, especially if their orders were to be disclosed so soon, but it moved the conversation on and took attention from the unfortunate new midshipman.

He might, after all, have been taught that sycophancy was the way forward and needed to unlearn. Mornington accorded William a nod before speaking.

"Alas no," the captain answered, "such opportunities rarely come for a mere Sloop of War! We did so well against the Americans however, we're to patrol off the Irish coast to prevent the bold rascals making a nuisance of themselves. We did what we could, gentlemen, but their

Lordships are still disappointed that we didn't take a schooner bigger than ourselves and far better manned than we as a prize too, and this patrol in the uncertain weather of the Irish Sea in Autumn is our reward for being bold but not quite as superhuman as their Lordships feel our poor efforts should be."

"The trouble is they're measuring the Jonathons by the standards we count for the French – that every English sailor is worth three Frenchmen" said William, dryly. "Since Americans are generally a specie of renegade Englishman they need to be given more respect. Especially as they won their War of Independence."

"Maybe nobody told the Admiralty that" laughed Mornington.

"To the Admiralty" Phrayle raised his glass "May their backsides never become as flabby as their brains!"

"Amen!" said Mornington.

Ffarquar looked shocked.

"May I ask, sir, what weather conditions we are likely to be sailing under?" asked Scully.

"You mean at your age, you've not sailed there?" interrupted Ffarquar.

Phrayle leaned over to cuff him across the back of the head.

"Last I heard, you're not the captain, Mr Ffarquar" he said. "I've never sailed in the Irish Sea either sir."

"Nor I" said William.

"Looks like we're all new to it then" said the captain. "Brigham?"

"Only once sir, but when you told me what was in the wind I asked around" said Brigham. "We're on the right side of Ireland, it can be wild in the Atlantic. Apparently even so it can hail at any time of year, though it's rare, and we're in the stormy season same as anywhere in England. I did discover though that the only time it's not raining is when the fogs come down."

"Joyous" said Mornington. "See that there are always irons in the galley fire for the men to dry their clothes by ironing them between watches if we have not dry out to let them blow, and have the purser issue an extra set of slops each. We can't afford to lose men to illness for never being dry. The purser is to issue rough blankets too to be kept below decks so the men can rub off the excess moisture on them; one to each mess, and the mess to be responsible for pegging them out to dry either between decks or if it's dry, on deck. Unless we're at battle stations I'll make it a standing order that the drying of clothes and bedding may be done any day that's suitable. It's still better than the West Indies, gentlemen; there we have to worry about mildew, black vomit and ague."

"That's God's own truth" said William fervently. "One can exercise and put on more clothing in the cold and damp; in the hot and damp you only wish you could strip off your very skin."

"Doubtless we shall have that to look forward to if we don't take enough American raiders" laughed Phrayle.

"No such luck" said Mornington "The Indies compensate for their weather conditions with some very nice prize opportunities – though they are rarely open to a mere sloop. Besides, we are not after prizes; our task is to run off any privateers that are wishful to raid Ireland and Wales."

"I can't see why they bother" laughed Phrayle "Nothing in Wales but Welshmen!"

Ffarquar went purple but bit his lip.

Scully chuckled.

"Don't spare my feelings about Ireland only having Irishmen sir" he said "It's several generations back and I've never been to Ireland in any case so I don't really think of myself as Irish, though my grandfather was keen to remind us all that he came over to work on the pike roads."

"I didn't know you were part Irish, Mr Scully, or I'd certainly have found a joke to make" said Phrayle. "I'm impressed at how well your grandfather did for himself; your father was a clerk too wasn't he?"

"Yes sir" said Scully "A clerk of works. He wanted me to study law. I'm glad to be in the navy though; wind, rain and fog cannot deter me, though it'll be tough on the topsmen."

"Indeed" said Mornington. "But we've some good hands; and they work well together. Mr Scully – John – perhaps you'll run through with the topsmen that haven't encountered stiff weather what to expect; looking at theory in this case is never the same as experience, but the old hands can share stories. Warn them not to scare the newer hands."

"Aye sir" said Scully.

"Sir, I should instruct the men; I have a background of generations of gentry; and I've read all about how to deal with different weather conditions" said Ffarquar self importantly.

"Yes lad, so has Mr Scully" said Mornington "And he's also assisted the topsmen when needed. We had to split the ships's company in two to take a prize you know; and most men and officers doubled up on the tasks they had to undertake. Mr Scully is experienced aloft so he can speak from that experience as well as from theoretical knowledge of weather. This is your first time at sea so I correct you with explanation. Do not ever try to contradict me again or you will be kissing the gunner's daughter for insubordination. DO I make myself clear?"

"Aye sir" said Ffarquar sulkily.

John Scully caught William's eye. This one was going to be a nuisance. He had noted William giving the brat the benefit of the doubt by drawing the captain's attention away – and how like Mr Price to be generous like that, he thought - but somehow he fancied that Mr Ffarquar was going to manage to gain attention regardless of help to deflect it, and would manage to antagonise even the most kindly officer.

Chapter 2

The other three midshipmen were used to viewing Scully in the position of dominie, helping them with their lessons, although they could technically, before, give him orders. This had been the means by which Captain Mornington had facilitated his warrant as it happened; having rated Scully in the books as schoolmaster, from which responsible position less questions wcrc asked over his application for a warrant.

 Scully had also helped the young gentlemen in a variety of ways, not least the avoidance of retribution for some of their milder pranks, which aid had been much appreciated. Colin Prescott, the main prankster, and little Peter Lord were quite happy to defer to him; and if Thomas Jenkins was less sure about how he felt at a former seaman now being his equal, he was certain that Scully was a better proposition to work with and even defer to than Mr Midshipman Ffarquar. Mr Midshipman Scully had some experience after all and was ready to admit to a lack of knowledge, making him, in Jenkins opinion, a bigger man than one who pretended more knowledge than he possessed.

Accordingly when Ffarquar grandly declared that at sixteen and with two years official sea experience from his three years in academy he was the natural leader of the Midshipmen's Berth since a man who had obviously failed his lieutenant's exams several times over as Scully must have done did not count, Jenkins turned to Scully.

"Mr Scully" he said politely "What do you advise that we do about this irritating person – ignore him or beat on him?"

"Mr Jenkins" said Scully gravely "When you knock the weevils out of your biscuit, do you bother to beat them or do you merely ignore them in a dignified manner?"

"I see; thank you Mr Scully" said Jenkins.

"How dare you!" cried Ffarquar "Do you have any idea of who I am? Will you listen to a jumped-up clerk whose grandfather was a labourer?"

"There's an odd sort of buzzing noise in here" said young Prescott "Sounds like a fly or something."

"This is intolerable!" almost shouted Ffarquar.

"Laddie" said Scully "If you didn't jump to conclusions and try to throw your weight around, the other lads would feel less inclined to act a bit childishly towards you. For your information I received my warrant late; I only applied relatively recently. I haven't done my full six years to be eligible for lieutenant's exams any more than you have. You have more technical sea time than I; but I have actual sea time. The most experienced of us all is Mr Jenkins who has almost three years sea time and in that time can still manage to prove when he takes his noon sightings that we are sailing atop the Ural Mountains in Russia. I am happy to defer to his sea experience where it is relevant; I suggest you do so too. However I am the one who is going to be making sure that you are up to scratch with your education because I am very well educated and I volunteered as boys' officer to free Mr Price who has been undertaking that office. So I would advise that you learn from this experience and try to think before you speak. This is a warship, not a boys' school with a bit of Naval tradition and you will not be permitted any leeway."

"Quite so" said Jenkins. "Shape up and shake down, Fartarse or whatever your name is. Mr Brigham won't take any of your cheek."

Ffarquar scowled but said nothing.

Scully resolved to keep a close eye on the boy and make sure that he did not decide to do anything to make him, Scully, look bad. It was not something he would put past the lad. He had no illusions that there were those who would try to make themselves look better by making another look worse, and an obviously spoiled brat like this, used to having his own way at home and perhaps having his way eased through the Naval Academy for parental influence and downright bribes, was likely to take any setback amiss.

This possibility was also on the Captain's mind and he spoke privately to William, Hector Phrayle and Brigham.

"That boy Ffarquar thinks himself something wonderful" he said "Keep an eye on him; he's the sort who is never wrong and has to find someone else to blame. He's also the type who will find John Scully's background too low to consider as anything but a convenient scapegoat, not to mention probably trying to bully Prescott and Lord. It's unfair on Jenkins, who is younger than the brat, and Scully too to have to keep him entirely under control so keep an eye out."

The two lieutenants and the master nodded.

"I'm bound to say Scully – Mr Scully I should say – has worked out better than I'd feared and is a credit to the uniform," said Brigham, "and I admit, I was wrong in my hasty judgement of him. Though I fancy Mr Price had a large hand in making his leadership skills work for the Royal Navy and not against it."

William flushed.

"Once I found out what he resented and why the rest was simple," he said, "with the kind assurance from the captain that he would do all he could. What's the news on the new hands?" he asked, eager to know what sort of quality of men they had received to replace those few killed and injured in the previous action.

"All volunteers thank goodness" said Phrayle "Nothing like a bit of prize money to get others willing to join. Only half a dozen but the old hands will quickly lick them into shape."

"An extra half dozen can make the difference in a gale" said Brigham. "Sail handling evolutions sir, to lick them into shape?"

"Yes," said Mornington, "and we'll continue with the competitions. I have managed to obtain some tea and chocolate as well as tobacco; I hope one of you knows how to turn tablets of chocolate into the drink."

"It has eggs and cream in it," said William vaguely, "at least my cousins Bertram drink it that way."

"Well it won't here" said Mornington. "No room for a cow on the 'Thrush' and the eggs from our few hens are too precious to drink."

"I've fixed chocolate before" said Brigham. "It has to be grated small to go into the water or milk it's made with, and the secret is in the whisking. I'll tell off the bosun to carve a cocoa whisk. That's a rare treat sir."

Mornington chuckled.

"I ran into someone who owed me a favour" he said. "A hot drink on cold wet days will be a welcome prize for the winners – and the quarterdeck too. I doubt it will go amiss to have a small slug of brandy in the chocolate too for the quarterdeck; for medicinal purposes of course."

Campbell laughed.

"As ship's surgeon I could only concur with such medicinal purposes if I tested the medicine" he said.

"Oh that goes without saying!" chuckled the captain.

One of the new hands was a tailor who had lost his job for taking part in some protests about the rate of pay fixed in 1795; well he was taking in consequence a considerable drop in pay, for though he would have his keep on board ship, a tailor might be expected to take home almost six times as much as a sailor earned. However his skills might as well be put to use, and Mornington rated him Sailmaker's mate – on some ten pounds a year more than as a landsman at twenty three pounds and two shillings per year – because it was foolishness to waste skills. And if the man had been something of an agitator, giving him less reason to have anything to agitate about would hopefully stop any trouble in its tracks.

As it happened the man seemed glad to have been given a new chance. He was unemployable in his own trade for having been labelled a troublemaker, and William noticed that it was not long before he was starting to make a little on the side by doing alterations to the basic slops the men got to make them a bit more stylish. Typically it was Scully who found out that it was not so much the pay that was the crux of the matter but the hours of work that in summer could be from six in the morning or before, to eight o'clock at night. He would work less sociable hours at sea, but not such long ones, as an overtired crew put the whole ship at risk. The wear of the ropes on the hands of a man used to delicate work would be cruel for a while but perhaps he would find the change of vocation worth it.

Especially if the officers, none of them wealthy, employed him to make up new uniforms at a slightly lower rate than the established naval tailors but still a nice bit of extra income to a sailmaker.

With his rather pedantic speech and reputation as a troublemaker the man, Kempe, was quickly dubbed 'Sew and Sew' by the rough wit of the men.

"We shall have trouble if we have to land" said Prescott as the ship beat against the prevailing winds westwards "When we're in the Irish Sea I mean; the Irish don't like us."

"Why don't the Irish like us?" asked little Lord idly.

"Because King John pulled their beards" said Prescott.

"That's a long time ago" said Lord.

"Well Cromwell wasn't very nice to them either" said Prescott vaguely.

"Yes, but nobody likes Cromwell" said Lord "Why should the Irish be more knacky about it?"

"Because – because they're Catholics and that gave the Puritans a pain in the whited sepulchre" said Prescott wildly. "And William of Orange made them stand in a pail."

"Why?" said Lord.

"Oh dear" said Scully "Colin my lad, your grasp of history is even more tenuous than your grasp of mathematics; it's a good job your seamanship more than makes up for it."

"All right Mr Scully, why DO the Irish hate the English? You have Irish ancestors so I suppose you ought to know" sneered Ffarquar.

Scully grinned.

"Actually I know because I went to a decent school where the Dominie made history an exciting story" he said. "The pale was a palisade to keep out the supposed barbarians and was from Medieval times, when the English in Ireland were inside it in Dublin to protect themselves . James II was thrown out of England for giving too much favour to Catholics in England and his brother-in-law was viceroy in Ireland. James went to Ireland and war broke out between Catholic supporters of his and the Protestant Irish."

"Oh are there Protestants in Ireland?" Thomas Jenkins asked.

"Yes, largely in Ulster; James I gave land to English protestants in Ulster to try to stop revolts and Cromwell did even more and disenfranchised the Catholics, took any rights from them to govern themselves that is" said Scully. "Anyway, William defeated James at the Battle of the Boyne – it's a river – and Catholics suffered penalties. Now just about the time Thomas here was teething, the Act of Union was passed whereby Ireland became a part of Great Britain."

"Didn't they like that then?" asked Lord.

"Well they might have liked it more if English landlords hadn't realised they could get more from their lands than they got in rents if they evicted their tenants and turned over the land to pasture" said Scully. "Thousands of people lost their homes and livelihoods and it's not really any wonder that they don't think much of the English."

"And would you turn traitor and support them?" demanded Ffarquar.

"Why? I'm English" said Scully "I can sympathise without thinking that fighting is necessarily a good idea; besides, it's the triumph of hope over experience. The Irish have never won by fighting the English. Catholics are banned from serving in the army or that would at least be a livelihood, but I've no answer. I only know that fighting will only bring retribution because the government fears revolution after the manner of America and France. But that's essentially the reasons behind the Irish dislike of the English."

"It seems fair enough" said Lord "If we have to land, we can maybe tell them that we don't want to take their livelihood away."

Scully laughed. The child was very earnest and very naïve.

And though Catholics were in theory banned from serving in the armed forces, Press Gangs did not take much account of religion, and a volunteer was worth three pressed men so nobody asked in the Navy.

He doubted they actually asked in the army either; from what he had heard a large proportion of the army in the Peninsula was Irish.

The idle talk of midshipmen could not of course be expected to last long when all the 'young gentlemen' were required to help with tasks surrounding a lot of sail handling, that beating against the wind required, changing every half an hour or so from the starboard to the larboard tack and back again. Then they were rounding the extended toe of Land's End and Scully wondered if he were the only one of the midshipmen if not of all the officers to whom the very land of Cornwall conjured thoughts of Tintagel, and Uther Pendragon, Arthur, Merlin and Guinevere. However such romantic thoughts did not get the courses shortened to prevent a gust from the Atlantic winds heeling the ship over as they came into the winds off the ocean before moving into the relatively quiet waters of the Irish Sea.

Chapter 3

The squall that struck the 'Thrush' as the ship rounded Land's End was sudden and severe, one minute fair skies then a yell from Brigham to lay aloft and shorten sail again, barely in time for the wisps of clouds he had seen in the West to have rolled into great black threatening thunderheads like, said William, the way blood dripping into water soon filled it with clouds of red like that fellow Macbeth.

"Cut yourself shaving this morning, Will?" asked Hector Phrayle. William gave a rueful laugh.

"Yes indeed I did" he said, screwing up his eyes as the first onslaught of the rain was an assault on his face' then he was narrowing his eyes, peering into the murk. "Sir! I think there's a sail, westward!" he added, scanning the horizon as best he might as the cruel lash of icy rain cascaded out of the lowering cloud.

"Mr – Ffarquar!" Mornington called, looking round to name the nearest midshipmen "Take the bring-em-near aloft and see what she is!"

"Aye sir" Ffarquar gulped. The prospect of climbing the rigging in the rain unnerved him.

"Use the lubber's hole, Mr Ffarquar rather than taking all day wondering if you have the nerve" said Mornington, not unkindly. Ffarquar nodded and started up the ratlines, glad of that permission.

Neither of the lieutenants mentioned that when they had been midshipmen such a permission would have spurred them into showing the captain that they did not need it, that they dared to climb out past the fighting top on the shrouds, hanging backwards over the sea.

Scully stifled a sigh. Ffarquar had to learn the hard way.

"Permission to go aloft sir?" he said "My eyesight's keen."

"Yes do, and give the men on the mizzen my encouragement while you're up there" said Mornington. "They're doing well but they look a little panicked."

"Sir" Scully reflected again what a good captain Captain Mornington was, to have noticed that. He grinned. As well to go up a different mast to young Fartarse anyway; the mizzen as good as any when looking to Larboard. He hated heights; but to climb aloft was his little victory over the fear. He took the climb one step at a time, and considered availing himself of the captain's permission to Ffarquar to use the lubber's hole. He was too mature to care about his dignity and the men knew he could use the ratlines if he had to. That was all that mattered; they knew they could respect his ability to perform as well as most topsmen. On the whole he decided to take the harder climb; the other young gentlemen would appreciate that he had managed where Ffarquar had not. Scully had not needed the lubber's hole for a long time, and though this icy lashing rain made climbing harder, almost blinding when peering into it, and the hands felt like frozen lumps of chewed bacon rind, he was glad that his fitness and hardiness was now such that he made good progress.

The men were surprised and deeply appreciative to have the captain's congratulations on their sail handling shouted to them as the wind rose to the sort of roar that made conversation nearly impossible. Catching even a glimpse of the other ship was hard in poor visibility but the sails flirted in and out of patches of heavy rain. He nodded to himself and scrambled back to the deck.

"You made an identification Mr Scully?" asked the captain.

"A tentative one sir" said Scully "I'm about eight chances in ten certain."

Mornington nodded.

"Good enough" he said. That was an accuracy estimate that was fair; not the nebulous 'I think so' which always irritated him. "What did you see?"

"Jonathon, sir; three masts, schooner rigged" said Scully laconically "Not as big as the one that got away."

Mornington gave a rueful half smile; he had the self confidence not to need to be the only officer to make jokes. He appreciated the concept of couching the comment in the terms of a fisherman.

"Well you know the type; I'd not dispute your tentative identification" he said "Let's see if Mr Ffarquar confirms it" he added as Ffarquar came damply down from the main mast.

Ffarquar saluted.

"Please sir, with all due respect, could Lieutenant Price not have been mistaken in seeing a ship?" he said "I could see nothing."

"Indeed" Captain Mornington bellowed relatively softly "And you, a raw hand who has never been to sea, sent to identify a sail think that you know better than the experienced man who saw it?"

Ffarquar flushed.

"The visibility is uncertain; it would be easy for him to be mistaken" he looked uncomfortable that the sentence had come out in something of a squeak.

"Mr Ffarquar; you are a fool" said Mornington. "I saw the sail as Mr Price pointed it out, as did every experienced hand on board. I wanted an identification of it, damn your eyes, boy, not a query as to whether the blasted ship existed in the first place or I'd have sent you to see if you could see a ship, not tell me what it was! What sort of little girls are they sending us from the Naval Academy that can't use a bring-em-near? Give it to me and go below to see if the gunner needs any help keeping the powder dry but for God's sake get out of my sight."

Ffarquar fled.

"Easy going is the Captain," murmured Hector Phrayle to William, "right up to the point some idiot argues on specious grounds to lay blame on others. Disagreeing with him he'll take – if you can put a good case – but trying to say some other fellow is mistaken he will not have."

"Little brat," said William in as much of an undertone as was practicable, "it wouldn't occur to me to doubt the word of a Midshipman, let alone a lieutenant, who said he'd seen a sail – even if I could not."

"A sensible Middy" said Hector, letting his voice carry to the straining and eager ears of the several eavesdroppers "Would confess to being unable to see it and perhaps advance the theory that either he knew too little to know how to look or that it had gone beyond visibility."

"Ffarquar you're a fool and a poltroon" said Jenkins "Letting the captain think we're all such little girls as to need the lubber's hole in bad weather, and not being able to do your job! You were representing the gunroom and you did a rotten job, what price your vaunted theory now?"

"I wager you'd not have seen a damn thing either!" said Ffarquar sulkily "If indeed there was anything to see! That Lieutenant Price made it up to get me into trouble!"

"Well of all the bounces I've ever heard that's the biggest!" said Jenkins. "It wasn't easy to spot and I couldn't tell from deck level and without a bring-em-near what it was, but I glimpsed it and so did half the crew at least; and Mr Scully went up the mizzen and got a tentative identification without a bring-em-near because it's an American Schooner, just the sort of thing we're on the lookout for, and one we've fought against together, Mr Johnny Raw. All I can say is, when we engage I hope the sounds of the guns don't make you sob into your handkerchee like a baby."

There is very little as bitter as the scorn of a fourteen year old, and Ffarquar flushed. Jenkins had an unfair advantage over him for having actually been into battle!

Mr Midshipman Ffarquar was beginning to realise that there was a big difference between knowing all the theory and actually experiencing sailing a ship in heavy weather and spotting and identifying sails in fleeting and transitory glimpses.

He was not however a youth who was willing to back down and admit that there were things he did not know; he preferred to lift a shoulder and turn away in a sulk. Jenkins shrugged. Let him; he'd either learn or the sea would kill him for failing to do so and small loss to the rest of them. A few years before, Jenkins would have been appalled at the idea of accepting with equanimity the loss of a shipmate to his own stupidity; but time at sea had inured him to sudden death and the idea that it was better for someone to kill themselves from ignorance than to manage to kill his fellows. The idea of Ffarquar surviving to become a captain made him shudder for the crew.

Still the boy might improve. After all had not Jenkins' own grandfather seen, when just a child, trained fleas harnessed to pull tiny chaises? It went to prove that anything was possible.

The weather was more miserable than particularly dangerous, so long as they kept well off the lee shore and stood towards Ireland. This was the direction in which the schooner had been seen to be heading in any case, so Mornington hoped they might not lose their quarry.

The rending tearing noise that rose above the sound of the storm heralded sudden disaster; and though Mr Brigham bellowed at the top of his lungs to get out of the way there was little else he could do but stand helpless as the upper half of the mainmast leaned inexorably with the awful creaking, cracking of doomed timber and like a mighty tree felled in a forest descended with awful slowness and inexorability.

One of the new hands had not got out of the way in time; and there would be a burial at sea, Sew-and-Sew would be earning his pay as sail maker sewing the man up in his own hammock, the traditional last stitch through the nose. He would also be replacing the topsail that ripped in half. The men worked feverishly to chop away the debris and to get clear the injured who might be treated by Mr Campbell.

"Weakened by time in the Indies no doubt" remarked Brigham "Lucky it didn't go when we were carrying all that press of canvas to outrun the Americans – or when we engaged them."

"I'll have a thing or two to say in Portsmouth about how well she was refitted" said Mornington grimly. "Yes, I dare say you're right. At least he wasn't a married man; but it's bad for morale, especially the new hands. Let's hope we can find that blasted schooner in this muck and give the men a battle to give them a taste of victory to cheer them up."

William was helping direct the clearing of the debris, and glanced at the remains of the mast.

"Well it's already been fished and woolded once," he remarked to Scully, "we'll have to put in somewhere to get a new one; and if we can't get seasoned timber, we'll have to jury rig a bit of tree to make do until we can."

"I suppose at least it prepares us for clearing up after hurricanes if we get sent to the Indies, sir" said Scully.

William laughed ruefully.

"One way of looking at it, anyway" he said. "Pity we hadn't had time for evolutions."

Scully nodded.

"I'll write to his mother if you like sir" he said interpreting that as William's regret for the death of the seaman.

"Good of you John; but I think the captain likes to do it himself" said William "Let him know that the man leaves a mother will you? He'll be glad that you've found that out."

"I shall. William" said Scully, appreciating the move from two officers to two friends for a brief moment, since William knew all there was to know about John Scully.

Scully's mother had died of an illness while Scully was in prison for an attempt at fraud to pay for her to have a doctor; he was sensitive to the relationship between a man and his mother, as the captain well knew. Scully was impressed that the captain liked to write letters to the families of dead seamen; very few captains cared to do so, even if they knew much about any seaman who had died. It was another example of Captain Mornington's care for his men beyond duty.

The men would like to know that, and Scully determined to pass it on. That would help morale.

If he ever became a captain, thought Scully, he would do the same. He suspected – correctly – that William had made the same decision.

"I've identified the coastline" said Brigham as they emerged from the storm into fitful sunlight "We've Waterford bay just north of us, and we can lay up safe there to do the repairs under the guns of Duncannon fortress."

"I've heard of that" said Mornington "Built originally to repel the Spanish Armada, I've heard that Boney was ready to pay good money for knowledge of its plans."

"Well we shan't have to worry about HIM again" said Hector Phrayle "The battle of Paris has seen the last of him; and his seapower long since decimated by Nelson at Trafalgar."

"Personally I shall only stop being concerned about Bonaparte when he's dead" said Mornington "It's a little more irrevocable than exile. William my lad, you may have the lads – and John for that matter – sketch the harbour and write a brief essay on its defensibility and defences."

William grinned.

"They'll almost be begging to do manual work replacing the mast in preference" he said.

"That was the general idea" said Mornington. "It won't do them any harm to look at theoretical questions with an actual example either. Might give Ffarquar a chance to show what he might be made of. If he can relate book learning to an actual site seen in good conditions and not under fire it would be a start."

"Aye sir" said William who somehow doubted that Mr Midshipman Ffarquar could manage to deal with a real example unless it was printed as a map.

Chapter 4

The fort was an impressive star shaped construction on a promontory into the broad estuary. The activity seemed excessive, and cannon were trained on the 'Thrush' as she came up to the mole to anchor. Apparently the garrison was sufficiently alert not to take any chances that a ship wearing British colours was indeed British. Bearing in mind the 'Thrush's' imposture in American waters this was not perhaps as outrageous a piece of wariness as might otherwise be thought.

Captain Mornington was met by a major with an escort.

"Major," said Mornington pleasantly, "we've put in to effect repairs; there's an American schooner about."

The Major relaxed at the soft west country burr just discernible in Mornington's voice.

"My apologies for all this, Captain" he said, indicating the vigilant troops with him "We've had a little trouble." There was a touch of the Irish brogue to his own speech.

"From that pestilential schooner?" asked Mornington.

"No, this is the first I've heard of it. Our trouble came from Irish rebels" said the Major. "Somehow they managed to drug a couple of sentries and get in to steal our Congreve Rockets; and I'm thinking that you should be apprised of that in case the devils try to use them against your ship. We've bolted the door after the horse is gone, I'm thinking. So there's a schooner about? D'you think they'd give the rockets to the jonathons to attack a fort with?"

"I wouldn't know; but to be aware there are rockets about is something to be prepared for" grunted Mornington, concerned. "Perhaps you'll give a couple of my brighter officers some pointers on the working of them?"

"Delighted!" said the Major, his face glowing with the joy of the single minded enthusiast.

Mornington turned to his quarterdeck.

"Mr Price, Mr Scully, you know about jury rigging, off you go and learn about rocketry for me and take enough notes to explain it to the rest of us later" said he.

The two men quickly murmured assent. William was delighted; learning more was always good! And that Scully felt the same way he knew. This should prove interesting even if it never came in useful. It would be too complex to write in a letter to Amelia – and since this had to be a letter to his sister, that Amelia would also read, would bore Fanny who would wonder why he should write about such things – so he must be sure to recall it well enough to describe to Amelia when he next had leave. William had no doubt that Amelia – Miss Finch he should say – would be fascinated. She had shown every interest in all aspects of the practical tasks of seamanship, indeed he had laughingly suggested that she would make a good midshipman.

He gave a wry private grin.

She would certainly make a better midshipman than Ffarquar. Although that was never going to be hard. William reflected that it was a bit tough on Ffarquar, doubtless a good scholar and finding the learning of facts quite easy, to be suddenly confronted with a taste of real life where the facts he was used to were not so easy to spot, and seemed as much use as trigonometry when casting the weekly accounts for, say, a pawnbroker, where the amounts were irregular in size as well as frequency and required the calculation of payments in more than one instalment. Both required mathematics.

At that, Ffarquar did at least appear to be well versed in mathematics and had made short work of the noon sights to date. His only mistake had come from a mistaken reading, and he had known enough to recognise that he had done something wrong and ask Brigham.

Brigham had been pleased enough that the boy recognised that he had made a calculation that would have landed them in the Azores that he has been quite patient with him in going over the work to see where the mistake had fallen. Generally Ffarquar was good enough at taking the sight, it had been the violent moment of the deck that had caused his error, having learned the use of the sextant on dry land. William had coached Scully in its use in the ship's jolly-boat which had bucked enough in the sound out of Portsmouth to emulate a larger vessel in heavier weather.

Ffarquar was actually enjoying himself sketching the harbour and writing an essay on its defensibility; although what he had no intention of confessing to anyone was that he found it much harder to work out from a real landscape than from the maps he was used to, the Board of Ordnance having excellent maps, copies of which were used in the training of Midshipmen-to-be at the Naval Academy. When the captain read the essays through later he was to note that Arthur Ffarquar was a sound and conservative tactician, that Thomas Jenkins had very little clue of how to relate the terrain to tactics although nobody could doubt he would make a fine seaman one day and a brave officer; that little Peter Lord had much to learn, which was unsurprising, but had a few good instinctive insights, and that Colin Prescott had a distinct flair once one had deciphered his execrable handwriting.

The Captain was later to share with his more senior officers that it had taken him a while to work out that a 'promingtree' was in fact a 'promontory' and that words he had taken initially as 'fart' and 'charnel' were indeed meant to be 'fort' and 'channel' which had explained a lot and had cleaned up his understanding of this singular and ink-bespattered document a great deal since the fart no longer overlurked the charnel, a more disturbing thought than the intended sentence that the fort overlooked the channel.

William laughed at that and remarked dryly that Mr Prescott's literary skills left much to be desired.

The repairs meanwhile progressed with efficiency while William and Scully learned of the mysteries of stabilising poles, charges, and the calculation of trajectories. Congreve had made a number of changes to his earliest designs, it appeared, based on those used by the notorious Tipu Sultan, that permitted a greater control of where they went, which as Scully remarked in an undertone to William was perhaps one of the more important features of anything that exploded. It appeared that the Navy had for a while toyed with the idea of mounting Congreve's rockets on ships but it had been found that they constituted a greater danger to any ship using them than to their target, since there was still a tendency for the rockets to veer to one side sufficiently to make setting fire to tarred sheets and the sails, even if furled, a very real danger. The decision had been rescinded, for which, said William, any naval officer should thank the Good Lord with devotion.

The Lieutenant who had been assigned to explain all about Congreve's rockets was a pinkly perspiring young man with a slight stutter; it was beneath the dignity of a Major to explain to lowly folk such as William and Scully, but William was soon making bets with himself over how soon it would be before the Major took over explaining his own pet enthusiasm from the unfortunate officer, as the senior officer was becoming more and more agitated over what he evidently considered an inadequate lecture.

It was an even shorter time than William had guessed when the Major exploded with a sound of wrath at a rather limp and lukewarm description of how rocketry worked – William thought it an unnecessary explanation as it seemed obvious enough to him – and charged in, waving the pink lieutenant aside to expound on such mysteries as burn rate of various fuses and how the explosive that provided the motive power must be contained save where the chemical reaction created thrust. The Major was enjoying himself, and judiciously worded questions from William and Scully probably elicited more information than he was authorised to tell, including the information that this fort had been testing an experimental version that had the guide pole screw mounted through the base plate rather than the standard guide pole mounted to one side.

Scully managed to gain an explanation of the different kinds of warhead to be delivered, from the simple explosive to the shrapnel and the incendiary. It turned out that the warheads stolen had been incendiary.

"If you ask me, Will," said Scully, as they returned to the industry that was the 'Thrush', "there's more in the effect on the morale from these rockets than any serious threat; from what I can see, if you are hit by one, it wasn't aimed at you."

"Tipu Sultan's caused enough trouble to our men in Mysore though, John" said William. "And the rockets led to the burning of the Jonathon capital of Washington."

"It's a little hard to miss a city" said Scully. "I have to say the idea that some half wild, desperate barefoot er, spalpeen of an Irish renegade has incendiary rockets is unnerving. Fire *is* the greatest threat at sea, and considering one coming near the powder store has me in a cold sweat. Is the captain going to hope to chase them down, do you think?"

"No idea" said William. "I'd think they would be more likely to use them against a political target on land though than against a stray sixth-rater like the 'Thrush'."

"You're probably right" said Scully "Sorry; too much imagination."

"Which will make you a great officer one day" said William. "Perhaps we should mention to the captain that stolen rockets could harass British shipping near the coast and make the chance of American ships having free rein much greater."

"You mean you hate the idea of them being in unauthorised hands and wondering where they might be pointed too" said Scully.

"In a word, yes!" agreed William frankly.

Captain Mornington took the possibility of incendiary rockets being used on British ships seriously; even one of such could cause serious problems for a small ship. It had also incensed him that the Colonel of the base had decided that tracking down the thieves would be too much trouble and would not be worth it, as the population would turn recalcitrant on them. The Major had seemed to agree with this assessment too, adding his scornful opinion that a bunch of unwashed ill-educated scum of Irish peasants would never be able to work them. Mornington was of the opinion that inexpertly wielded rockets were twice as dangerous as those used well, even allowing for the thieves not being particularly knowledgeable.

"Mr Scully, how many of the crew do you know are skilled poachers?" he asked.

Scully considered.

"Not as many as if they had volunteered not been pressed from gaol" he said dryly "Successful poachers don't get caught. But four to my knowledge."

Mornington nodded.

"Any man may be subject to bad luck" he said. "Ask them if they'll volunteer to track thieves who might burn us to the waterline. "

"Sir" said Scully. He approved of Mornington's policies of letting the men know why they were undertaking such tasks as they were set; it made them keener.

It certainly made him keener and all men were alike in liking to know why they might be risking their lives. He called over the four poachers, two from Essex, one from Lincolnshire and a Welshman, and outlined what they were to do.

"And what are we to do when we find these ruddy paddies, look you, Mr Scully?" asked the Welshman.

"Report back, Taffy" said Scully "The Captain isn't expecting you to have to apprehend them, he knows you're not marines."

One of the Essex men spat over the side.

"Reckon him'll be glad ef we use our noddles and see what's what" he said in a slow, countryman's burr. "Ef they be down a hole, then ferrets in red jackets be needed to ferret un out, else we moight hev a charnst to bring un in. We'll do as seem right, Taffy me lad and never moind arstin' arter orders."

"No direct orders, Peacock" said Scully "The Captain knows you lads can be trusted to use your heads and not to risk them neither."

Peacock spat again.

"He's a damn good captain" he said. The others murmured assent.

The poachers were glad of a bit of shore leave away from the hard work of replacing the top mast; and there were several conversations with them before they left regarding various messes putting shares into any coneys that found their way into the hands of the said poachers. William had very little doubt but that there would be rabbit stew on the menu, and doubtless too the poachers would be curing the skins to protect them from the bitter weather. He had no idea how they might set about that and thought regretfully that if it smelled as bad as tanneries usually did it would have to be vetoed. He mentioned as much to Hector Phrayle.

"Oh, they'll taw them with alum" said Phrayle "Salt and roll them until they can get some like as not. My uncle was in the glove making business" he added by way of explanation. "Tawing fine leather for gloves and curing with the skins on is a different business to tanning. I could welcome a good rabbit stew. I let them have cord to make good snares."

"Ah, the wardroom's share" laughed William.

"Oh absolutely" said Phrayle "And John Scully's arranging their shore time the gunroom's share. I fancy everyone else is paying in tobacco."

William chuckled.

The dynamics of shipboard barter would have to be seen to be believed by a landsman!

The poachers would be setting their snares as they tracked their quarry; and collecting anything they caught on the way back. If they also caught human thieves they might not manage to collect rabbits as well; but that was yet to be seen. William certainly did not doubt their ability to find where the Congreve rockets had gone, he had heard his uncle on the subject of the evil genius of poachers too often to consider their tracking abilities likely to be deficient.

Whether they came back with rockets, rocket thieves or neither was in the lap of the gods.

William dismissed idle speculation from his mind and went to shout at a hand who was employing an adze with more enthusiasm than skill and called to the carpenter to show the man once again how to do it properly. William was glad that Miss Finch was not on board since the names the carpenter was bestowing on the unfortunate sailor were outside even of William's vocabulary and he had heard plenty in his six years afloat.

He stored them away for future reference.

One never knew when colourful epithets might come in useful. At least the ubiquitous Mr Lord, whose relatively angelic appearance concealed his insatiable curiosity about things he described as 'smutty', was currently mastheaded for having been caught attempting to introduce wood shavings into the top of Mr Ffarquar's breeches when the older boy's shirt had come adrift for bending forward.

Chapter 5

The new top mast had been swayed up and fixed into place before the poachers returned, and Ffarquar had been voicing his opinion that all would have been found to have 'run'.

Thomas Jenkins had told him not to be such an idiot.

"They won't run, they trust the captain" he said "and besides, what's to run to? A hostile countryside with no good living to be made? They aren't daft. I take it that you won't be partaking of any rabbit stew when they come back?"

"There won't be any; they aren't coming back" said Ffarquar stubbornly.

"Right, all the more for the rest of us in the gunroom" said Jenkins.

The other two boys nodded; and Scully gave a mental shrug. Ffarquar must learn for himself the code the lads lived by.

The stew was to be mixed game as it turned out; the poachers had a full bag of coneys, several woodcock and a brace of partridge. Hector Phrayle raised an eyebrow as they came over the gangplank.

"Don't ask, sir, look you" said Taffy.

"Perhaps as well not to" agreed Phrayle. "A couple of you report to the captain and the other two report to the cook."

There were rather blackened grins. By common consent Taffy and Peacock were to make a report while the others headed for the galley, gathering those who had volunteered services plucking, skinning and drawing as their share.

Mornington regarded Peacock and Taffy with an encouraging expression.

"See it's like this, sir" said Taffy

"Give over Taff do, and don't be orl them owd day singin' to him about it you Welsh idiot" said Peacock "He can't help all that squit sir, his bonebox sprang a leek."

"Better than being a mangelwurzel head like you, look you" retorted Taffy "I'll tell it in my own way and the captain iss a fair man, and ready to hear it from someone who doesn't murder the King's English like you."

"I'll hear from one at a time or both of you will be in trouble" said Mornington firmly. Peacock sniffed but nodded to Taffy to continue.

"We followed the trail of those *ach-y-mochyn* paddies" said Taffy "and look you, a child unbreeched could have done it, for they were not used to travelling with heaffy and awkward equipment. *Ach-y-fi*, lubbers" he added scornfully. "Well they were long gone when we reached the end of the trail, Captain, and *Duw*! Were we surprised! For take it from me, Captain, we neffer would have expected to come upon a ship, cutched down in a quiet valley, like, when we cocked over that last fence, we were taken aback were we not, Adam-bach?" he appealed to Peacock.

"We wus whoolly slumguzzeled" said Peacock nodding agreement, being used to Taffy's colloquialisms. "There it wuz, large as life and twice as threatenin', Mr Price's schooner ef I don't miss my guess and what price anyone not being able to see it *now*" he added in satisfaction.

"Leave any insinuations against my officers out of it" said Mornington sharply. Ffarquar might not have the respect of the men but he must still be backed up; and the men would treat him with the respect due to the uniform or Mornington would have to punish them.

"Not meanin' any disrespect sir" said Peacock instantly, realising he had gone too far. Mornington nodded acceptance of what was the closest he was going to get to an apology.

"And the schooner had loaded the rockets?" he said.

"Indeed, look you" said Taffy "And they were busy with a fire fixing to make some kind of a frame to fire them from. *Duw, duw*! And planning to fire them at the houses of parliament too, the devils, though there's nobody in there will be a great loss, still it iss an insult, Captain!"

"Good God!" said Mornington. "You heard them say so?"

"Yess indeed" said Taffy "One of them laughed and said 'the English parliament will haff a shock when these come through the windows' and what else would he be meaning?"

"Indeed" said the Captain. "One for each of you......" he took four guineas from his pockets. Taffy and Peacock grinned. That was an unexpected extra reward!

"Will we sink the schooner?" asked Peacock.

"We'll certainly deal with it" said Mornington grimly. "Show me if you can on the chart where it was."

This necessitated a little discussion, but the countrymen were adept at reading the land once Mornington had explained some of the conventional symbols on the map. They had to follow their own route overland to get there, but Mornington was patient, and nodded as they traced their way to a small river, no more really than a creek, that snaked back and forth well enough that activity upon it would not be obvious from the sea.

This would require some planning.

"This will only work if the Schooner is still there" said Mornington, outlining a plan to sail down the coast, and land some of the ship's guns onto the mouth of the estuary where the schooner lay to give plunging fire while the 'Thrush' held station at the mouth of the river to fire on her also and prevent her from leaving. "The men took two and a half days to return across country; I am gambling on the fact that if they are making proper metal A-frames to fire the rockets from that will take them some considerable time. They don't want them to shake apart or they'll risk their own ship more than the target."

"It's risky enough firing those damned things from shipboard any how" opined Brigham.

"Granted; but offered the opportunity to burn London in exchange for the burning of Washington, I cannot see that they would be able to resist" said Mornington "I would not, in their shoes. Equally I would want that gesture to be as effective as possible, and not to lose the initiative by having my rockets shake themselves off the A-frame and put themselves out in the Thames, or worse, do nothing but burn my own rigging."

"Sir," said William, "rather than land guns to enfilade her as you have suggested, to sink her, might it not be a greater victory if we landed boarding parties under cover of darkness, as close as possible, while the majority of the schooner's men are engaged wooding and watering for the forging of the A-frames? We might take the scattered crew in detail, or even just board the ship and sail her quietly away."

"You forget one thing in the quietly sailing away" said Mornington. "Taffy said that the rockets were still on the shore, which to my mind is a sensible thing on the part of any captain, who does not want infernal devices, filled with such noxious things as sulphur, to be on his ship longer than is necessary. We have two dozen thirty-two pounder carcass rockets to deal with too; it was an heroic effort on the part of the Irish rebels to carry two each, I have to say, it's a weight any man can manage, but very awkward and ill balanced."

"They are the smallest carcass rockets" said William "But it was a clever choice, for the next largest, the forty-two pounders, would need to be carried individually and that would be less firepower. The range on the smaller ones is still close to two miles, well three thousand yards, which is sufficient to cause a lot of damage and still have the chance to run for the sea, after having fired them at the heart of London. But might we not use tactics of stealth so far as they are concerned also? On this chart, Peacock has drawn a rough shelter, where I conjecture they are kept; there will be a sentry to deal with, but our poachers, led by someone who knows the construction of the rockets, might empty them of their charge and the incendiaries in the carcass, and duly carry that away without ado, rendering the rockets inert. They might then be collected and returned to the fortress once we had finished the business of taking the schooner and rounding up her crew."

"Potentially hazardous," said the Captain, "for those dealing with the gunpowder and the incendiary devices that is. Are you volunteering?"

"Like a shot, sir!" said William.

"Very well. Mr Scully will be your second in command and the poachers under you. Take them right now to the fort and get that pink idiot to let you take some apart in broad daylight. Mr Phrayle, you will be in charge of the main boarding party, Mr Brigham, you will lead a secondary shore party to cover Mr Phrayle taking the schooner. Mr Price can be given the gist later; he has an urgent mission to learn how not to blow himself up!"

William grinned as he saluted and left, collecting Scully and the four poachers.

He told them what they were to do.

Peacock spat.

"Blow ourselves to kingdom come I shouldn't wonder," he said gloomily, "my ma said I'd hev a bright future but reckon she didn't mean as a yuman Chancel-match."

"If we get it wrong it will be as spectacularly unpredictable as Chancel's friction match" said William "Which is why we are going to do our best not to get it wrong."

He decided to ignore the whispered comment that 'the Yankee wench' which he presumed meant Miss Finch, might want Mr Price hot, but not crisped to a cinder.

It was more dignified to pretend not to hear.

The pinkly-perspiring lieutenant was not happy at all but when William suggested that he might ask the Major instead the man capitulated and showed William and his coterie how to dismantle the rockets. If his manner lacked enthusiasm for the task – after all he would have to put them back together himself, not trusting sailors to the task – he was at least attentive and efficient at the matter.

He had no desire to be blown, in Peacock's idiom, to kingdom come either.

"So, why do you want to know how to take them apart?" he asked curiously.

"Oh, the captain reckons he knows where the rebels might have taken them and on the offchance that we should find them, he prefers us to carry back the charge and the warhead separately" said William, easily.

Scully darted him a look but said nothing.

"Nervous type, your captain" said the pink lieutenant, in a superior sort of voice.

"Very cautious, any way" said William, equably. "Likes to minimise the risks."

He did not say that the captain minimised the risks of operations that most other captains would consider far too risky even to try. The pink Lieutenant laughed scornfully.

"Your bad luck" he said "No prize money in the offing – no wonder he got a tedious job like patrolling the Irish Sea!"

William just shrugged; and Scully kicked Peacock in the ankles when that worthy opened his mouth to extol the captain's virtues.

Peacock took the matter up when they had learned what they had come to learn and had left; and asked,

"What for did you kick me, Mr Scully? And what for did Mr Price run the capting down?"

"He didn't" said Scully "He let the lieutenant do so however for a very good reason" he looked at William.

"I get it, look you" said Taffy "They let the *Ach-y-fi* things be stolen in the first place and Mr Price is of the opinion that it might have been more than a bout of carelessness-like as led to the rebels getting in."

"I shouldn't necessarily go so far as that," said William, "though one cannot discount the possibility. But they have been shown to be careless and if that lieutenant should go talking about what we are really up to in front of servants, well who knows how far it will go."

Adam Peacock spat.

"Sorry sir" he said gruffly "Loose lips means a tight hempen collar — leastaways, that's the way we puts it where I come from."

"We may not be likely to be stabbed with a Bridport dagger," said William, using the naval slang for being hanged, the best rope coming from Bridport, "but if those Americans get wind of what we're up to, we'll be in trouble."

Chapter 6

Captain Mornington hugged the coast, thankful of fair weather; there was enough north in the wind to make it possible to avoid tacking and just sail close hauled, and with the aid of the chart and the memories of the poachers he put down William and his party a short way up a creek that necessitated a man at the leads to check if the 'Thrush' had enough water under her. 'Thrush' would sail past the end of the narrow entrance to the estuary where the American was lying to drop the other boarding parties. On due consideration Mornington had decided not to send Brigham off ship, as the sailing master was invaluable, but had placed young Jenkins in charge of the second shore party. Jenkins, proud as could be, was supervising the putting of the sharp onto his men's cutlasses.

"And the captain a brave man indeed" said Hector Phrayle as he shook William's hand as the latter prepared to depart.

"In what way particularly?" asked William.

"He's keeping Ffarquar with him" said Phrayle, gravely.

William laughed. It was true enough to be a bittersweet joke though; and bitter for young Ffarquar. But he would be a risk to the mission if sent with Hector, and not likely to lead the second mission one tenth as well as young Jenkins. William would certainly have requested not to have him in his party had the captain suggested it. Of course without such experience, Ffarquar would not have the chance to learn, but he really only had himself to blame for that in being singularly inept and completely at sea, at sea: as one might say.

William certainly doubted he was any better at practical tasks on land either.

He was not that sanguine about his own skills on land, at least so far as this mission was concerned.

He knew the poachers would roll their eyes at him and at Scully for being unable to slither soundlessly and almost unseen into the available cover and told Taffy to take the lead as the most experienced man at such important matters.

Taffy nodded and took it as his due; keeping up a low commentary of how to read the land and avoid leaving too many signs oneself in the hopes that the lubberly officers might at least learn something.

Not that he said so out loud, but the implication was obvious. William took no offence; the man had some justification.

They passed a hovel where the smell of a peat fire lay rank on the air, a barefoot man and his threadbare and barefoot wife and children tilling a pitifully small plot of land, gathering in the first of their meagre harvest of potatoes. The peasants glanced idly at the passers by with that dull incurious look of those too careworn to take much notice in the doings of others. Scully's breath hissed in.

"At that they are better off than those turned off their land" said William quietly.

"Mr Price" said Taffy "Can I ask you something?"

"Ask" said William "I shan't take a genuine enquiry amiss."

"These poor devils… what for are we fighting them when they are so needy?"

William sighed.

"A complex question, Taffy. And we are not really fighting them. Some of them fought us by taking the rockets. Can I blame them? Not really. But they gave those rockets to our enemies, the Americans. What mismanagement there has been in Ireland is not our business – unless any one of us should find himself in Parliament, which is unlikely. However, I fancy that with the history of brutality towards the Irish over the last few hundred years, even if Parliament addressed the issue and gave back the land to Catholic Irish families that is owned by Protestant families sent in to Ireland, there would still be dissatisfaction. For those who were English and went to settle now think of themselves as Irish and would not wish to be displaced, and so they would be the ones fighting instead. And I make no doubt that there would be those who want to fight for revenge and others who mistrusted any who wanted to redress wrongs. In my opinion there will still be trouble with Ireland in another two or three hundred years."

"It seems unfair, look you" said Taffy.

"Unfortunately a lot of things in life are" sighed William. "All we can do is to do our best to do our duty; and hope that those in power know what they are doing."

He decided to ignore the sniff from Peacock that indicated that the Essex man thought the idea of anyone in power knowing what they were doing was extremely unlikely.

The going was tough.

William found that after getting his sea legs, walking on land was actually extremely uncomfortable; and he was besides not used to walking any great distance. Covering five or six miles over rough country was unpleasant in the extreme; and he knew Scully was suffering too. He caught the junior officer's eye, and a shared grimace was sympathy given and accepted. The ex poachers seemed to take it in their stride, quite literally however, so neither officer was about to make any comment.

The fact that loose trousers were more comfortable for walking in than breeches did not help, but officers and gentlemen were not supposed to complain. At least they need not be ashamed of the appearance of the ship's company on shore; Captain Mornington was one of those who insisted on a uniform, with some regard to individuality, with indigo drill bell-bottom trousers and matching woollen jackets, white shirts and the sailors' choices of waistcoat. Some of the waistcoats were things of great beauty, patiently embellished and embroidered by the men, proud of their uniform but proud too of their individuality. Taffy had decorated his nankeen waistcoat with knotwork, turk's heads worked to make buttons, and a selection of knots in dark blue cord running down the waistcoat in stripes; Peacock, true to his name, had embroidered peacock feathers on a blue waistcoat of *serge de Nimes* that the sailors called denims. The other two, Jackson and Walden, had respectively a linen damask waistcoat and one with stripes embroidered on to plain nankeen. Jackson was poor at stitchery but good at bartering. Concentrating on that, thought William, made the painful journey go quicker.

The hedges were at least gay with pendulous red and purple flowers. Scully stopped and peered closer.

"I thought so!" he said "They're fuchsia; my mother had one in a pot that I bought for her. They must have been brought to Ireland by the land owners and run wild; well I never! Will, two minutes?"

"Certainly John" said William casting himself down on the ground, short turf nibbled away by rabbits well enough drained that it did not feel so very wet. Scully felt about his person and extracted a sheet of paper from a pocket.

"Mr Lord's Latin exercises" he said "I'm sure he won't mind donating it to the interests of science."

William laughed.

"Especially if it's bad enough that being used as such will get him out of trouble!" he said.

"Oh it's not too bad" said Scully, deftly folding the paper to make a cup and scrabbling earth into it. He nipped the ends from some of the fuchsia plants and pushed them down into the earth. "I heard tell that they grow readily from cuttings; just a reminder of my mother. The landlord had thrown away everything while I was….away."

William nodded and touched his friend on the shoulder once he had scrambled up again, not sure if the brief rest had helped or had made resuming the walk harder. Scully had only committed fraud to try to help his mother, and she had died while he was in gaol for it. William was not about to come between him and any memento the man might see in this plant. How broken tips of the plant might grow without roots he had no idea, but he was not about to cast any dampner on John Scully's joy.

Who could say that it might not grow? William had no idea what a cutting might be, but Scully seemed to know what he was doing. William hoped the plants would grow. If they could survive being aboard ship. If they could not, perhaps his sister would care for any that survived for Scully.

It made another small thing to think about besides his aching feet and the chafing of his small clothes as they trudged through the failing light of the crepuscular gloom that came on so rapidly at this time of year.

He asked Scully about Fuchsias, and learned that they came from South America and had been brought to England by a sailor some twenty years previously and had rapidly become popular with flower fanciers.

"A bit of country in the town, a pot of fuchsias" said Scully "They grow well in pots, though you'd not think it seeing these wild things, almost trees some of them are. Mother like her fuchsia. Had me find out all about them for her."

William wished deep down that he could feel as much affection for his mother as Scully felt for his; but when he had been home on leave last, staying there, not the brief visit he had made before this mission, he had been appalled by how little discipline the younger children had, and how Susan was left in charge by his parents.

She would have a better life taking Fanny's place at Mansfield Park as a companion; quieter too. And she would be near Fanny and that would be nice.

190

He heaved a sigh of relief as Taffy dropped back and whispered urgently,

"Sir, we're nearly there, ready to conceal ourselves until it's properly dark look you. But there's something-like you need to see, *duw, duw*, it issn't what we expected."

William's heart sank; maybe the schooner had already gone. That meant valuable time would be lost in getting all the boarding parties aboard again before going in pursuit; and she was a faster ship. All that could be done would be to use the telegraph from its most westerly station at Plymouth, to warn London of her approach. That might prevent her from bombarding Parliament with Congreve rockets but he could just imagine the court martial – some sarcastic captain asking why Mornington has not gone in immediate pursuit and rubbing salt into the wound that Captain Mornington thought that they could capture the schooner instead of sinking her. And that it had been Lieutenant Price's idea. Mornington would never say so but William knew he would have to speak up.

And then he was wriggling on his elbows beside Taffy, with the confounded fuchsia flowers dropping from the hedge down the back of his neck, to look over the small natural harbour.

The schooner had not gone.

There was now a second schooner there.

William swore softly.

"Aye sir. That's what I thought sir" said Taffy.

"All right" said William "Do you think you can find Mr Phrayle and his party?"

"Aye sir" said Taffy. "They're as noisy as cackling-cheats look you and less useful for they do not lay eggs, the noisy lubbers... not Mr Phrayle of course sir" he added hastily.

"Damn your eyes, Taffy" said William.

Taffy grinned. He knew that William meant that he knew full well that Taffy thought the officers to be singularly useless at field work and rebuked him for showing it, though without taking much offence.

"Sorry sir" he said.

"Just watch that clever Welsh tongue of yours" said William. "Go to Mr Phrayle and tell him – er, suggest to him to decide which schooner he plans to take. We'll deal with some of the rockets by putting them into the other one once he's under way. If he thinks that a good plan."

Taffy grinned again. Officers evidently had to be careful what they said about or to senior officers too.

He disappeared into the twilight like a ghost leaving William wrestling with plans about how to deal with this unexpected situation and fears that Hector, a good man but not over burdened with imagination, might want to make his own plans.

Chapter 7

William kept an eye on his watch, glad of the sliver of waxing moon to show him the hands, though Peacock had muttered darkly about any moon at all, even so weak and feeble a sickle as this. William had retorted that had there been a new moon and total dark, the likelihood of being noticed was increased by the ineptitude of the non poachers of the party who knew their limitations and would like to get out of this alive by using the fading beams of the setting moon to get them into position around midnight, intending to be ready to begin the engagement at moonset, about two in the morning.

Peacock's grumbles had subsided.

Having his officers fall over their own feet would not be a good thing, and the jonathons seemed to be pretty lax in keeping watch in any case – at least to landward.

Peacock granted grudgingly in his own mind that approaching by land had been a good idea and Mr Price at least could think like a poacher even if he walked with the grace of a cow with falling sickness.

Taffy had returned with news that Mr Phrayle considered Mr Price's idea a good one and had told Taffy that he planned to take the schooner that had arrived first as all her hands seemed to be displaced and that would give them more quickly and easily a second fighting ship if need be against the other. William concurred and was glad that Phrayle had thought that through and had not decided to go for the one nearest to the sea. Moreover, the second schooner was anchored in the middle of the river, and there were comings and goings by boat; the first appeared to have found deep water by a hastily constructed pier.

He ceded the lead to Taffy again, he and Scully bringing up the rear behind the sure-footed poachers, trying not to make any noise, and copying the actions of those ahead of them assiduously, dropping to the ground to proceed further by means of the elbows for the last few hundred yards. William pulled a rueful face over what it might be doing to his uniform coat and to Scully's; outfitting did not come cheaply, even second best uniform for everyday wear. Well, the prize money from the taking of the privateer 'Mosquito' and the cargo she was carrying would help there. He also wanted to spend four guineas on David Steel's two volume work 'The Elements and Practice of Rigging, Seamanship and Naval Tactics', a vital work for any young officer with ambition, but a very expensive outlay.

They had reached the foreshore now, and were out of any vegetation; weed squelched horribly under William's reaching hands and he hoped fervently not to put his hand on any jellyfish stranded at the high water mark. Though not so vicious as those which could be found in the tropics, even small and long dead jellyfish could give an unpleasant sting to the unwary palm. Apart from the pain, which was to be avoided, an inadvertent cry would not be good. Hastily he warned Scully in an undertone.

Scully nodded; and Peacock, who had looked irritated at first at talking by the officers, also nodded.

"Spit on it if y'do find one, sirs," he added quietly, "'twill ease the sting."

William nodded thanks rather than be vocally courteous; he wondered if as well as poaching, Peacock had been involved in a little 'bottle fishing' on the side in the quiet backwaters of the estuarine rivers of Essex where he might have been likely to have found out a means of easing the discomfort by personal experience while waiting to collect a cargo of liquor and lace 'run' by smugglers.

The rockets were stored above the high springs mark of course, but Taffy was leading the group by a circuitous route to take advantage of the lie of the land. William trusted him to know what he was doing and tried not to let his hand cringe away from its encounters with the detritus of the deep.

Then Taffy was rising near the looming shape of a structure whose presence was more noticeable by the absence of stars where it occluded them than by its shape as such; the thin moonlight flashed bright on a blade and a stifled gurgle marked the demise of the sentry guarding the rockets.

So far so good.

Lieutenant Hector Phrayle had also been taken aback by the second schooner; and to say that he was pleased when one of William's party of poachers slithered out of the undergrowth with a suggestion from the younger officer was an understatement. Will had worded it diplomatically too; Hector was not a jealous man of nature and he recognised with a little wistfulness but no resentment that William had what it took to be a fine captain one day. He confirmed the plan with Taffy, deciding that the ship that had been emptied of crewmen was the better prospect to be taken and sending the Welshman back with a message to that effect and hoped it had been what William would have planned.

Young Mr Jenkins and his party were still with Phrayle – Captain Mornington had not trusted him not to get lost and had suggested both parties stayed together until within sight of the objective – and Hector Phrayle communicated to the boy what was to happen.

"Your part has not changed" he said "Harry those who are likely to try to stop us taking the schooner, and regroup and meet the 'Thrush' on the headland where hopefully you will be joined by Mr Price and his party. Your only additional instructions are not to get in the way while Mr Price deploys the rockets."

"Aye sir" said Jenkins, wishing he had had the foresight to volunteer to learn rocketry. His task was the least exciting of all – no rockets to fire, no ships to board, just lead the sailors and the marine contingent under a sergeant in causing mayhem to allow Mr Phrayle to sail away and maybe not survive to be picked up again. But then that was the lot of the junior officer; to be expendable. And if he did his job well, Mr Phrayle would appreciate it because he was that sort of man. He depended on Jenkins and his men!

Hector Phrayle smiled; he had a good idea what was going through the boy's head.

"I'm relying on you, Mr Jenkins" he said. "I know you will make taking that ship possible."

"Aye sir!" said Jenkins, coming to attention to salute before leading his own party off to get into position.

The crew of the first schooner were largely camped ashore, being concerned with the matter of wooding daily to make the furnaces to build the A-frames, which were stacked, three completed, at some distance from the hut full of rockets, between them and the main body of the men, who were currently sitting round a fire apparently eating stew cooked on it while some of them took turns to sing or play various instruments. They were not expecting trouble, at least from the land; though a sentry was on a high point and sang out that the Limey sloop was passing on to the south. The majority seemed to have settled down to enjoy what they were seeing as shore leave, and were quite careless that they might be overlooked by unfriendly eyes.

Indeed, they had lit a roaring fire and were engaged in cooking a late supper over it, with much backchat and horseplay from those not actually cooking. It made approaching quite near an easier task, and though neither the poachers nor the two officers were about to take risks it was good that they might reach where the rockets were stored with a likelihood of less risk.

William opened the door of the rude storage hut – or rather lifted away the hurdle that served as a door – and he and Scully looked in at the two dozen potentially lethal rockets.

"How many will we fire at the schooner and how many will we dismantle sir?" asked Scully.

"If it needs more than four to destroy the fighting capabilities of the schooner, we are obviously so inept that another score would make no difference" decided William. "Taffy, Peacock, Jackson, Walden, the A-frames are over there; if you can move one without alerting the men there at their supper on the shore and bring it nearer, do so; if not, tell me now and we'll build a sand hill to launch from. Well, mud and sand" he amended.

"Safer sir" said Scully "Besides, then what we dig out if we go down as well as up can act as a berm between us and the rest of the explosives."

Peacock spat.

"I ain't sayin' it can't be done, sir, but it'd be a tidy bit o' work and tedious difficult" he said. "It'd oony take one o' they Yankees to take it into his head to take a leak over near the frames and we'd be spotted – or he'd notice one gone."

William nodded. It had been a stupid idea to want to move the frames – and showed how much he could himself be a victim of conventional wisdom that dictated A-frames to fire rockets. It was as well that his men were independent of mind and would tell him when they felt that his judgement was flawed. He recalled that he had once heard someone say that only a small man had need to hold an idea tenaciously if it were shown to be false, that a man who could modify his thinking was more worthy of respect. William hoped that his men would respect him for taking their word and not think him merely vacillating. As it happened, his men were relieved to have an officer, in Peacock's idiom when they discussed it later, who 'knew a B from a battledore and had the sense t'know when he were barkin' up the wrong tree afore draggin' everyone inter trouble behind of him'.

"Very well," said William, "I'll go with your judgement. You find yourselves digging instead."

Jackson was heard to mutter that if he had intended to till the soil he would never have become a poacher and ended up in gaol in the first place; and Taffy poked him.

"Shut it, you, and concentrate on winning us a nice piece of prize money in all that head money look you – and in helping take the other *ach-y-fi* schooner."

Jackson subsided with a sniff.

Digging down was better, William had to agree with Scully, it made their excavations less obvious. The sound of singing and the scraping of an ill-tuned fiddle helped to cover any noise they made; and the Americans, staring at their own fire, had their night vision destroyed for the time being. William disapproved; in enemy territory, and knowing that an enemy sloop was passing by, Captain Mornington would have forbidden singing and playing, knowing how well sound might carry over water at night. However the cock-sure confidence of the American captain in permitting it was in the favour of the crew of the 'Thrush'.

William and Scully both utilised sextants to measure against the height of the target schooner's mast to make a reasonable estimate of her distance. They would need to know this to calculate the angle of the slope from which to fire the rockets to get the right trajectory; and William had decided that if there was a discrepancy he would go with Scully's calculation.

There was no significant discrepancy fortunately; and the sextant was again in employment to measure the angle of the slope.

This was the only vital thing about the construction of the firing pit; and William left Scully supervising, and called Taffy to help him disable the other rockets. There was only room for three men digging and one to supervise in any case.

"Nervous business, look you" said Taffy conversationally.

"Yes and that's why we're doing it" said William "You see yourself as the leader in your quartet; and I'm in charge of the mission. To the victor the spoils, but only if he takes responsibility."

"Iss that so?" said Taffy "*duw*! We haff the good officers on the 'Thrush' to take risks with the men, look you, and it's honoured I am to take risks with you sir."

"We're a good company" said William. "And let's keep our minds on the task in hand not to need the final services of Sew-and-sew."

Taffy gave a low chuckle.

"Lieutenant, *bach*, if we needed his services ofer this, there'd not be enough of us left to scrape into a hammock, let alone it being likely to find a nose to put the last stitch through!"

William had to agree with that sentiment.

The black humour of the British sailor carried them through many a bad moment; and he had to confess that he would be glad when all the rockets were separated from their charges and the incendiary warheads.

"There's a boat pulled away from the one we're turning into a bonfire sir" said Taffy quietly.

William looked; a jolly boat was pulling towards the shore.

"Tell the others to keep their heads down; these new comers have their night vision" he said.

Taffy slithered off like an eel.

Silently they watched the boat come ashore and an American officer, walking stiff legged with outrage approached the other ship's company.

He pulled the fiddle from the grasp of the fiddler and threw it at the fire – fortunately for the owner he missed – and addressed them.

"Captain Tyrell wants to know what the blazes you idiots mean by making all this row; don't you realise there's a British warship out there? It may only be one of their wretched little sloops but dammit! There's no need to let them know that we're here! Even a limey captain on one of those tubs knows the difference between an Irish folk song and 'The Eighth of January'. Now keep it quiet!"

With which pronouncement the officer stalked off.

There was a pause before a few cautious whistles and hoots of derision rang out.

"Well!" said Scully quietly to William "That says to me that the second schooner has a more prestigious captain than the first and he has shoved his oar into the whole business."

"Indeed" said William. "Well, we have an hour to go before Mr Phrayle will attack so we'll just have to finish in silence. These Yankees look to be readying for their sleep in any case."

Chapter 8

The sliver of moon had disappeared behind the rest of Ireland and two rockets were set up to launch. It might have been a wiser decision to have sent one off as a ranging shot; but William made the choice to have more noise and confusion with two. Moreover, if the second schooner was alive to the danger, assuming her captain to be more canny than the rather slipshod, over-confident captain of the first schooner, getting a second shot at her might be a matter of guesswork in any case.

William's ears strained. Did he hear the sounds of muffled violence from on board the first schooner? Was that a brief cry, cut off, or was it a night bird? That was surely the squeak of blocks – yes, the sails were coming down, the capstan was working, the ship was about to get under way.

The further she could go without it being noticed from the shore or by the second schooner the better; and with the apparent contempt in which Tyrell of the second schooner held his colleague there was a good chance he might think it was merely some whimsical devilry of a man he plainly disliked.

All of which could buy Hector Phrayle some time.

It was to be hoped that Mr Jenkins and his men would not be needed; though he had his orders to suppress the Americans and kill or capture them as he might once Mr Phrayle was under way if at all practicable. William and Scully would assist with that too if they might do so without jeopardising their mission to bring back the rockets' contents; though William had an idea that would enable the return of the rocket bodies too.

The schooner was out in midstream by now, and Hector making every use of the current to take him downstream, perilously close to the other schooner, but Hector knew what he was doing; there would be no collision.

Hector's prize was being hailed now from Tyrell's ship; William wished that he might have brought a telescope, but there had been no question when he had left the 'Thrush' of using ordnance so he had not included one to watch for fall of shot. It had only been a last minute decision to take his sextant, because it might come in useful. It had indeed done so.

There was a hail of sorts from Hector's prize; it sounded truculent and William hoped that Hector was making reply of the kind 'mind your own business'; since Hector too would have seen the friction between the two crews.

And now there was a cry from one of the seaman ashore, mostly sleeping but one more wakeful sailor noticed what was going on, and gave vent to an inarticulate ejaculation of surprise then a question about where the 'durn ship' was off to.

The other men were waking, fuddled from their first sleep, staring in bemusement, unsure what to do.

The second schooner was weighing anchor, the starlight enough to show the water glinting as it ran off the cable.

"Very well, Mr Scully, you may fire at will" said William. He was glad that his voice remained steady and neither shook nor squeaked. He had been half afraid that the nervous dryness of his throat would betray him when he spoke!

Scully nodded.

"Aye sir" he said.

They had kindled a slow match in the pit, where its firefly glow would not be seen by the American seamen; and Scully applied it to the fuses of the rockets, leaping agilely back and vaulting out of the pit to be well away from the back blast. The little flame climbed the fuses like demonic sailors going hand over hand up the rigging and then disappeared within the rockets. There was a long moment of anticlimax.

Then with a hissing shriek the rockets spat flame from their tails and leaped into the air propelled by that fiery tail uncoiling into the ground and howled their way overhead.

"Lumme!" said Peacock, and spat. Taffy leaped into the pit to stamp any sparks out and Scully jumped down beside him ready to set up the next two rockets.

"Send 'em lower" said William his voice shaking slightly in excitement. "They're going to hit the sails!"

"That ought to enliven the night" said Scully dryly, kicking at the slope to make it fall to a shallower angle. "Have to be by guesswork, Mr Price."

"Guesswork will be perfectly acceptable Mr Scully" said William trying not to giggle with nervous elation.

Meanwhile the sailors from the first schooner were realising that one or more of their own rockets had been fired. The cries were largely of confusion, then a voice shouting 'Traitors! Benedict Arnolds!' among them convinced them to start to move towards the pit.

"I hope Mr Jenkins hasn't gone to sleep" muttered Scully.

"He'll be there" said William "Young Jenkins is dependable – has a good sense of timing too."

The words were no sooner said when a fusillade of shots rang out and a large number of the sailors running towards William and his party dropped in their tracks.

It was probable that in the environment they knew, the American sailors were as calm as any in battle, and capable of taking far heavier fire without flinching. Awoken in the dark, in the unfamiliar terrain they found themselves, unsure what was going on, whether their captain was sailing away from them, and with their own stolen rockets in use a sufficient proportion broke and scattered to make it easy for Mr Jenkins and his men to mop them up in detail.

And Scully was ready to set the slow match to the next pair of rockets.

"I'm not sure I got the trajectory low enough sir; I'm sorry" he said.

"With luck it may be compensated for by the fact that the schooner is now under way and has increased the range" said William.

The hissing scream again, and the glowing red parcels of fire, fear and death hurtled through the night. There was the sound of an impact; and then the night was ripped in two with a flash from the schooner that was followed within heartbeats by a thunderous detonation that shook the earth and made the watching British sailors stagger on their feet. A fireball ascended, spreading out like a common field mushroom of smoke and fire and heat.

"*Duw!*" said Taffy.

"Dear G-d!" said William.

"Must have hit the magazine" said Scully, awed. "Let's hope none of the burning debris has hit Mr Phrayle. Are we going to join Mr Jenkins?"

"Yes" said William "And I thought we could hamper the prisoners he's taken by making them carry the carcasses of the rockets so we can take them back too."

The American prisoners were inclined to be truculent and making them carry the heavy metal rockets seemed a good idea to young Jenkins too. The gunpowder and the incendiary powder were carried separately in barrels by the four poachers; the barrel staves and rings had been brought by William's party in a collapsed state for easier carriage and were a simple matter to put together, with a few curses from the men on the cooper when they found any of it heavy going. Jackson was busy relating a story of how, when buying butter in just such a firkin, one should ask to have the staves removed to check the colour all the way down for consistency and to see that nothing smelled rancid; the point of his discourse being to point out how funny it would be if anyone wanted their brand of butter exposed.

It was not especially funny but the others laughed in relief.

"You'll not mention what's in the barrels in front of the prisoners if you please lads" said William "We don't want any of them getting ideas."

"Nossir" said Jackson "They'm out o' earshot."

"They are or I'd have checked you earlier" said William. "Be careful though."

They nodded. The American prisoners outnumbered their captors and Jenkins only felt half safe by tying their right arms across the middle of their backs by the expedient of tying right wrist to left elbow. They could get each other out of it but it made things harder for a concerted rush to be organised, especially then hampered with the rockets. The wounded had their wounds to contend with and that made for a potentially dangerous, but fairly well controlled group of prisoners. And William was in charge of them, being the senior officer. He spoke to the sergeant of the marines and reiterated that the marines were to shoot to kill if the prisoners looked as though they were trying anything on. The sergeant nodded stolidly; such orders were no more than his own inclination. However having the orders from a superior too meant that he and his men could not be blamed for anything.

William was to be glad he had given the order towards dawn, when in the greying light half a dozen of the Americans dropped their rockets and made a run for the bushes.

The Marines opened fire with alacrity; one of the Americans fell, and the rest may or may not have been hit as they dived for the bushes.

"Some of you are going to be carrying more rockets thanks to your friends" said William.

"No limey; you'll be carrying them for us!" said one of the prisoners "Up and at them lads, they've discharged their weapons!"

William cocked his pistol.

"I haven't" he said.

The prisoners hesitated.

The American ringleader sneered.

"You can only kill one of us" he said.

William placed the barrel of his pistol to the touch hole of one of the rockets still being carried.

"Would you care to place a wager on that?" he said.

The man's face drained of colour visibly even in the dim light.

"You wouldn't" he said "You'd kill yourself too!"

"Better than being court-martialled for losing you" said William "Besides I say my prayers regularly so I don't fear death. I'd rather avoid it however and a court-martial so how about you agree to behave and pick up one of those rockets?"

"You cold-blooded, misbegotten son of a gun!" said the American.

William shrugged.

"But I do have skeletons in the closet of my ancestry too" he said.

The American laughed reluctantly.

"We'll play it your way you devil" he said.

William let out his breath quietly. If they had only known it was a bluff!

He was less happy when it came to distributing the dropped rockets to find that six men had gone but only four rockets were on the ground.

They had taken two deliberately, probably on the principle that it was all they could reasonably manage. Well if they tried to fire them they would have a surprise, but he must make a song and dance about it.

"Sergeant!" he said "There have been two rockets taken by the escaping prisoners! Take a couple of men and follow them – do whatever you have to do."

"Yessir" said the sergeant, looking worried. He was not privy to the disabling of the weapons. "Budd, Chitterling, Snape – with me."

The three men fell out and William kept his pistol cocked as he waited for them to return.

It was a tense period.

The bushes parted and the sergeant emerged.

"I'm right sorry sir" he said "But I think they may have been helped by rebel Irish who could have been tracking us. They've vanished into thin air. We didn't dare go on, for fear of falling in the bogs that seem to abound" he added. "Apart from the one we killed before he got to the bushes there's one more dead and one bleeding but it's enough to carry the rockets away especially with local aid."

"Then let us hope that you are wrong and that they have fallen into a bog" said William, working on sounding somewhere between irritated and concerned. "Drowning those wretched rockets ought to put them out of action."

"Yessir" said the sergeant woodenly "But I think they were led across it; they had not had time to sink and I thought I heard voices. And there was blood leading into it."

William frowned.

"Well I shall place in my report that you did your best" he said "They are not easy weapons to use; the rebel Irish are more likely to blow themselves up than anyone else and a bunch of privateers that are little better than pirates hardly likely to do much better. Let's get along; I want to be back on board."

The sergeant nodded; he could not see how he might track the missing rockets over the bog in any case, but he certainly hoped that Mr Price was not being too blasé!

He felt a lot better when William beckoned him to the back of the cavalcade and explained concisely why he was not unduly concerned!

Chapter 9

By the time it was fully light, the shore party and their prisoners had reached the small cove on a headland where the 'Thrush' was to pick them up; and indeed the 'Thrush' was there waiting.

It was as though the arrival of the prisoners was a signal, for the nasal twang of an American voice sang out a single word:

"FIRE!"

Up the slope on the headland and overlooking the bay were a motley crew of ill-clad Irish and the surviving escaped prisoners. They appeared to have the two missing Congreve rockets with them.

William hoped that the boats setting out from the 'Thrush' would reach the shore before the prisoners realised that the rockets on the headland were not firing.

He moved closer to Scully and nodded to him to close up towards Jenkins and the marines; the poachers missed nothing and would follow their lead.

None too soon.

"Hey, those rockets aren't working! They're empty! And he knew it all along!" It was the same spokesman William had managed to subdue by threatening to fire into the touch hole of the rocket.

The Americans flung down their burdens, and though hampered with their arms tied made a concerted rush – and they were aided by the onslaught of a ragged band of Irish charging down the hill.

"Mr Price sir!" cried Taffy, hurling the barrel he was carrying at the oncoming mass of men.

William grinned and sighted. His pistols were not duelling pistols from Mantons but he was fairly certain that he was a good enough shot to hit a firkin.

He fired, and dropped.

The resultant explosion was all that could be hoped for, and William swore as a piece of flying, burning debris cut painfully across his cheek.

His own band had followed his lead and dropped to the ground, but as they were closest to the explosion they were the ones most at risk form it, and it had not seemed to have done more than minimal damage to their own marines who were firing and then using their muskets as clubs; one of the prisoners had fallen from a wound to the back of his head from a piece of flying barrel. And sharpshooters from the ship were opening fire; it was extreme range but they seemed to be aiming over the heads of the party fighting on the shore to at least keep the heads down of any Irish who had not been blown up by Taffy's timely barrel.

William, trying to rise, found a charging American almost on him and almost instinctively grabbed for a handful of sand to throw up into the man's face. It made the attacker flinch back and William took the heavy service pistol by the barrel and whacked it hard into one of his assailant's knees. There was a nasty cracking sound and the man fell with a scream of agony.

William felt a little sick. This desperate hand to hand combat was a far cry even from a boarding action. He flung the heavy pistol at another assailant as he rose and wished he was wearing a sword. Taffy handed him the stave of a barrel; they had taken apart the other barrel of gunpowder to have some kind of makeshift weapon. A barrel of gunpowder was, after all, only of use as an offensive weapon when it might be cast far enough away to only damage the enemy. William laid about him. How slowly the boat was pulling to the shore! Surely it must arrive soon!

The melee was confusing and all William could ever later remember was hitting out left and right, Scully at his shoulder, and little Jenkins down and sobbing in pain behind them. And then the assailants were decreasing, were gone, as the marines in the boat leaped out of it into shallow water and finally, assured steady ground to make each shot tell, were firing into the enemy.

William left it to then to put irons on the surviving captives; he went to Thomas Jenkins.

"Tom lad, where are you hurt?" he asked.

"My shoulder Mr Price" gasped Jenkins "One o' them damned Yankees hit me with a Congreve rocket!"

William winced.

"A nasty wound" he said "Shoulders are damnably painful…. Hang on there lad, Mr Campbell will see to it soon. Here, let me tie it up for you and take the weight off it" he added looking round for something to use for a sling.

The shirt of a dead American would do as well as anything else and soon Mr Jenkins was looking slightly less green.

"Well Mr Jenkins, if you must go castin' up your accounts," said Peacock, "at least it's only on the bully beef and biscuit we brung with us, not good coney stew!"

Young Jenkins managed a shaky laugh at that.

"Damn your eyes, Peacock" he managed "I wager you forgot to snare any more on our way back here."

"Well sir I confess it didn't occur t'me to set snares what with those blasted Yankees and the rockets to see home" said Peacock.

"Well nobody can think of everything" said Jenkins with an attempt at a grin.

William was glad to be back on board the 'Thrush'. The captured schooner was, he discerned as soon as he was back aboard, standing out to sea.

The poachers were being made much of for their description of the use of the rockets.

"*Duw*, the first ones were a sight enough" said Taffy "Bursting in the air with their hellish red glare."

"Was that meant to rhyme?" asked Able Seaman Peters. "Keep at it Taffy and maybe you'll write a song as well as singing with your speech – that there was almost poetry."

Taffy said something short and ugly in Welsh that did not need much translation.

"Well it was when Mr Scully set off the magazine that it was more nor a red glare, it was like the gates of Hell had opened and the devil himself spitting flames" he said.

Most of the men had never seen a magazine explosion and listened with horrified fascination.

The story grew with the telling and so did the size of the explosion until Scully came up to the group Taffy was telling the tale to and said quietly,

"And I'm told the one that got away was big enough to swallow Jonah."

"Mr Scully sir! Are you accusing me of telling fisherman's tales?" said Taffy in self righteous indignation.

"Just pointing out that you're heading in that direction" said Scully.

The sailors who were envious at having missed all the fun grinned and turned to teasing Taffy for his exaggeration.

It may be said that Midshipman Ffarquar stopped sulking about not being the midshipman sent to lead the men of the ancillary shore party when he discovered that Thomas Jenkins had sustained a nasty and painful wound. The shoulder had been broken and it would be many a long day before the youth was fit for duty again. Young Jenkins cried more bitterly over the news that he would be invalided out for the time being when they reached shore than he ever did over the pain.

The return of the rockets and their incendiary warheads was a moment of sweet revenge for the dismissive attitude of the Major at the Fort. His stunned silence was music in William's ears. And when they told the story of what had been done, the pink lieutenant who had so despised Captain Mornington for his supposed caution looked ready to burst in outrage.

"I told you he was a cautious man, our captain" said William to him.

"But – but that is outrageously risky!" spluttered the lieutenant "Not cautious at all!"

"No?" said William, preparing to strike a blow for the Navy against the army. "Perhaps it's just the way sailors look at it; I'm sure you people who have fortresses measure caution by a different level to the way we do at sea."

It was the closest he could come to calling them a bunch of cowardly poltroons without having to fight a duel over it; and William had no intention of fighting a duel. He had enough enemies of his country to fight without wasting time in a fruitless battle against a supposed ally just because in his opinion, which he felt was justified by the facts, they were lax in their duty and lacking in zeal.

The schooner carried some supplies to be condemned as a prize and she would be a trim ship for the navy to buy in, as were all the privateers. However it was the head money that would bring most to the crew this time. At that, nobody had expected any prize money for a routine patrol.

On due consideration, Captain Mornington called Mr Phrayle back to the 'Thrush' and dispatched the schooner, 'Dancing Dorothy' by name, back to Portsmouth under the command of Mr Ffarquar and as slender a crew as he could get away with. None of them would be likely to see the 'Thrush' again; they would swiftly get made up on the roster of other ships in harbour. So too might a midshipman of sixteen years old trusted with a prize; and any captain who shipped him only finding his mistake later. That at least was how Mornington put it privately to Phrayle and to William.

"And I never said so" he added.

"If the boy gets a posting as second lickspittle to the flag lieutenant on a first rate he might do well enough" said Phrayle. "I hope you sent someone with the ability to get him there with him?"

"Yes, the gunner's mate" said Mornington.

William and Phrayle both chuckled. The gunner's mate was an experienced enough petty officer but given to grumbling and to having sudden ailments when hard work was indicated.

Young Mr Jenkins was also with Ffarquar, capable of standing a watch for him just until they made landfall, good enough to check his navigation and in need of hospitalisation. He would be missed.

And William had sent a long letter to his sister and through her to Miss Finch; who would deplore no doubt the violence involving her countrymen but would be interested in such details as the fuchsias. William had plucked a few blooms and pressed them between the leaves of his pocket book, and enclosed them. Fanny would find it fascinating too that so exotic a flower should now run wild in the hedgerows.

By the time they returned to England after this patrol it would be winter fairly; and they might then hope for the chance to go to the Caribbean.

In the meantime he somehow doubted that the rest of the voyage would be as exciting as this first part!

.

Naval Glossary

This is by no means a comprehensive list but covers the terms used in these first two stories about William Price.

Accommodation ladder A portable flight of steps down a ship's side

Aloft: In the rigging of a sailing ship.

Amidships aka midships: In the middle portion of ship, along the line of the keel.

Anchor: metal object with hook like arms to engage with the seabed and prevent drift attached by a line or chain raised and lowered by the capstan

Anchor's aweigh: the anchor has cleared the sea bed

Articles of War: the regulations. Read by the Captain when first coming aboard as part of 'reading himself in' and to be read out every Sunday to remind the crew. Article 36 '…and any other crime not covered……' was known as 'the captain's cloak', there to cover the more ingenious mischief of the British sailor, but could be abused.

Astern: towards the stern (rear) of a vessel, behind a vessel.

Athwart: At right angles to the fore and aft or centerline of a ship

Avast: Stop, cease or desist from whatever is being done.

Aweigh: Position of an anchor just clear of the bottom – ie its weight on the cable not resting.

Back and fill: To use the advantage of the tide being with you when the wind is not.

Beam: the width of the vessel.

Beating aka Tacking: sailing as close to the wind as possible on a zig zag course in order to sail essentially into the wind.

Beat to quarters: to beat the signal on the drum to go to quarters, ie to be in position to fight the ship.

Belay: [1] To make fast a line around a fitting, usually a cleat or belaying pin. [2] or to secure a climbing person with a line. [3] An order to halt a current activity or to countermand an order previously given.

Bight: A loop in a rope.

Binnacle Where the compass is situated.

Bitter End: the last part of a loose cable or rope. The anchor cable is tied to the Bitt, a post at the bow, and when all the cable is paid out the bitter end has then been reached.

Block: a pulley.

Bosun aka Boatswain: warrant officer in charge of ropes, sails, rigging and boats who uses a pipe to send commands to the men and may 'start' or hit them with a cane if they are not fast enough.

Bow: the front end. ['the pointy end']

Bow chaser: a gun pointing forward for use in pursuit.

Bowsprit: Spar extending forward from the bow used to secure the forestay and other rigging

Bulwark: The part of the ship's side extending above the upper deck generally to about waist height of a man.

Cable: A heavy rope.

Cable length: a tenth of a nautical mile.

Capstan: A winch operated by capstan bars that fit into it that sailors may push against walking round the capstan to lift the anchor or winch other heavy objects. In small vessels floggings usually took place with the offender lashed to the capstan.

Cat o' nine tails: the nine ended whip used for flogging. Each was made for an individual punishment and placed in a red baize bag, leading to the sayings 'to let the cat out of the bag' and 'not room to swing a cat'.

Caulk: driving oakum into the ship's seams which is then covered in tar to ensure that she is watertight.

Close hauled: sailing close to the wind, ie with the wind on the quarter [side] of the ship and the sails adjusted to get some modicum of forward motion from it.

Course: Lower or main sail

Dunnage: personal baggage

Figurehead: The identifying carving set at the bow beneath the bowsprit representing the name of the ship.

First Rate: the largest 3-masted ships of the line with more than 100 guns and a crew of more than 800.

First Lieutenant: the position of the lieutenants was decided purely on the date of their commission, ie when they had passed as lieutenant. The first lieutenant was the senior officer under the captain and his right hand man.

Fish: repairing a mast or spar with a fillet of wood which may then be woolded, wrapped with cordage for extra strength.

Forestay: long cable from the bow to masthead to hold the mast

Furl: To roll or gather a sail against its mast or spar.

Gaff: spar holding the upper edge of a fore-and-aft rigged sail

Go about aka tacking aka come about: to change direction from one tack to another by going through the wind

Gunwale: upper edge of the hull

Gybe: To change from one tack to the other away from the wind, with the stern of the vessel turning through the wind. The command 'gybe oh' is given.

Hardtack aka Ship's biscuit/bread: the unpalatable staple hard and long lasting biscuit

Hawse [hole]: the hole in the side of the bow through which the anchor cable passes.

Heaving to: stopping a sailing vessel by the expedient of using the helm and setting the sails in opposition to each other to stay as stationary as possible.

Helm: the wheel used to steer the ship.

Holystone: the chunk of sandstone used to scrub the decks, named partly for its size and shape that was similar to a church Bible, and partly for the kneeling position in which it was used by the sailors as though in prayer.

Junk: old cordage past its useful life. Picked over for oakum to caulk [seal] the ship's seams.

Jury rig: verb or noun, to rig a temporary repair of a mast or spar and sails when the original is damaged, to use to sail to a place a proper repair can be effected, refers too to that temporary rig.

Kiss the gunner's daughter: slang for bending a boy over a gun for a caning

Larboard: obsolete term for port, the left side of the ship, used for such things as the larboard watch.

Lee: the side in the shadow of the wind

Lee Shore: a shore towards which the wind is blowing, ie it is risky to manoeuvre close to it for fear of being blown onto the shore unless the vessel handles well to windward.

Leeward: the direction towards which the wind is blowing.

Letter of Marque [and reprisal]: a document awarded to a privateer to condone certain acts of piracy as acts of reprisal against enemy vessels

Lubber's hole: Space between the head of the lower mast and the inner edge of the top. An alternate route into the top of the futtock shrouds for the timid climber rather than climbing over the edge of the top using the shrouds. It was considered unseamanlike to use it.

Lubber: dweeb

Mainmast: the tallest mast.

Mainsail: the lowest and largest sail on the mainmast.

Mainsheet: control line that most controls the trim of the mainsail.

Master: captain of a commercial vessel, or when Sailing Master the highest warranted rank on board ship in charge of navigation and day to day running of the ship.

Master and Commander: an obsolete position still used in colloquial description of a lieutenant commanding a ship. On board he is 'the captain' but his rank is still 'Lieutenant'. By the time of William Price the appointment was just 'commander'; like commodore it was an appointment not a formal rank.

Masthead: a small platform part way up the mast just above the main yard, where a lookout is posted whence men working on the main yard will gather and thence go about their duties. Being mastheaded – sent to the masthead – was a minor punishment for midshipmen, less for any danger or unpleasantness as for being banished for a while and probably missing a meal. In cold weather one would get cold and stiff.

Mess: a group of crewmen who eat together; also the place were they eat.

Mizzen Mast: the hindermost mast on the ship. [technically the third mast but this was often the third]

Nipper: short length of rope used to attach a cable, that is too large to be itself by the capstan, to the 'messenger' or rope moved by the capstan, to draw the cable along with it. The job of attaching this rope was in the purview of the ships' boys, hence the term 'nipper' for a small lad.

Orlop Deck: the lowest deck above the hold, it is below the waterline. Here the surgeon performed any necessary operations.

Port: Lefthand side.
Prow: the pointy end aka bow.
Purser aka pusser: warrant officer in charge of victualling and other supplies. His perks were the buying and selling of slops [clothing] and luxuries like tobacco at a profit. Pursers had a reputation for corruption and some certainly provisioned with poor goods in order to pocket the difference between the permitted cost and what they actually paid.

Quarterdeck: the aftermost deck, the preserve of the officers.
Quarter Gallery: toilets for the use of the officers.

Rates: the means by which fighting ships were classified. A first rater had over 100 guns and 800+ crew; a frigate would be a fifth rater, 36 guns, 300 men; the smallest war ships were sixth raters, a dozen or so guns and about 40 men.
Ratlines: rope ladders permanently rigged between bulwarks and tops to permit access to tops and yards.
Rigging: the system of masts and lines permitting the manipulation of the sails.

Scarfed aka scarphed: a joint to wood when jury rigging to extend a broken spar, in which both pieces are partially cut back to be lapped together.

Scuppers: drainage pipes and channels to channel any water coming inboard out through holes in the bulwarks.

Scuttlebutt: the barrel with a hole cut in the lid for a dipper, set at the foot of the mainmast where water was freely available to the men [except in times of water shortage]; that the men would hang around gossiping gave the name 'scuttlebutt' to rumour and speculation.

Sextant: an instrument used to measure latitude.

Sheet: a rope used to control a sail in relation to catching the wind.

Shrouds: standing rigging from the masts to the ship's sides.

Sloop: A small warship, sixth rater. Very difficult to define as the Navy Board seemed to define by the work it undertook more than any particular configuration.

Slush: the grease scooped off the top when cooking the meat. First call on it was from the Master and bosun for greasing blocks and parts of the running rigging, any surplus was the cook's perks to sell or barter. Essentially it is dripping; and made the ship's biscuit less unpalatable if spread on it.

Sounding: checking the depth of the water with a sounding line weighted with a lead weight. Sounding leads had a hole in which wax could be inserted to bring up a sample of the bottom to check what comprised the sea bed.

Spar: the wooden pole used to support the sails and various rigging.

Starboard: the right-hand side.

Stern: the back, or blunt end, of a ship.

Sternlights: the large windows across the rear of a ship generally giving onto the maindeck giving light to the captain's cabin.

Swinging the lead: Skiving. when sounding, the lead needed a good heave to get it to go a decent distance, but this being tiring work, someone who was just swinging the lead was skiving.

Tack: to move on a zig-zag course to enable some progress against the direction of the wind.

Under way: moving in a controlled manner.

Vang: a rope holding the boom from riding up on a fore-and-aft rigged sail, or a rope securing the gaff to the ship's rail.

Watch: a period of the day during which a part of the ship's company are on duty; watch also refers to the division of men, generally being known as the starboard watch and the larboard watch.

Wearing Ship: tacking by turning away from the wind.

Weather gauge: Favourable position over the enemy sailing vessel with respect to the wind; having the opportunity to get the jump on them.

Woold: more a carpentry term, the use of old [stretched] cordage to wrap around a fished or scarfed joint to strengthen it in jury rigging.

Yard: the horizontal spar from which a square sail is suspended.
Yardarm: the end of the yard.

4036031R00131

Printed in Germany
by Amazon Distribution
GmbH, Leipzig